A LOVE STORY

BY

JULIA CYNTHIA KENT

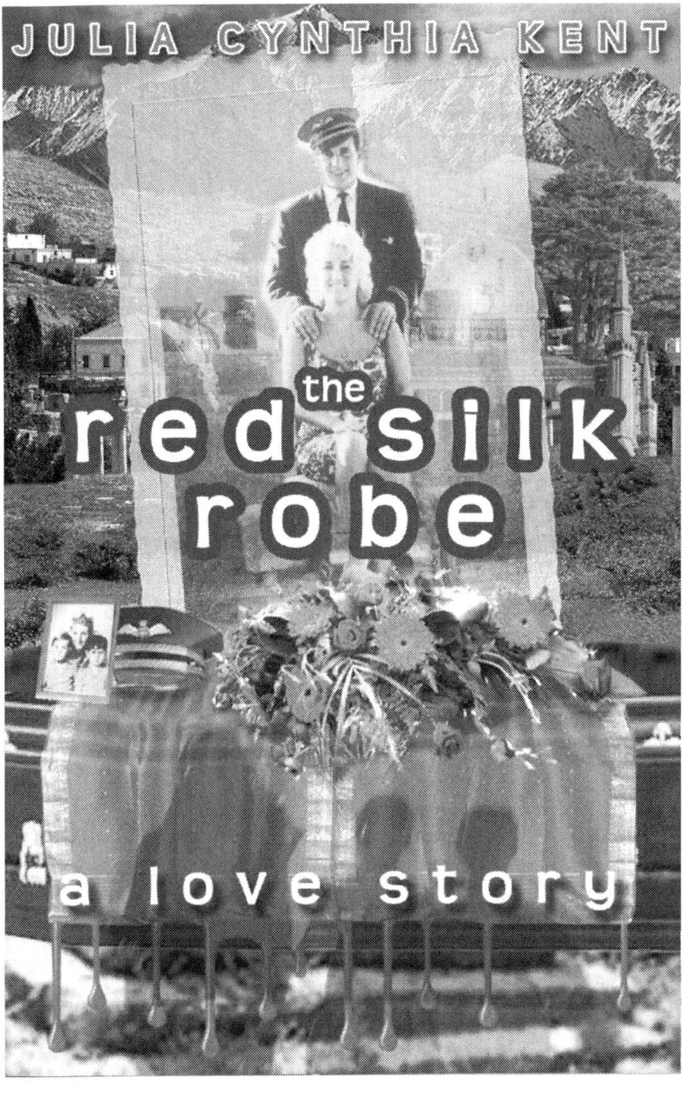
JULIA CYNTHIA KENT
the
red silk
robe
a love story

The Red Silk Robe
is a true dramatic story of
an English dancer, singer/showgirl; her travels,
her destined and fatal meeting with her
Lebanese love, her escape to England
to save her children from her Moslem in-laws
and the final exit from war-torn
Beirut to Dallas.

AUTHORS NOTE

I acknowledge that most of the first names used in the Red Silk Robe book are real. The surnames have been changed for protection of the innocents, but everything in this book is true and authentic... so help me God and Allah.

There is nothing meant to be anti-Moslem in the Red Silk Robe; these are the facts as I lived them. The authorities enforced the law as the Koran states;

I was just lost in the crossfire of love and religion....

I dedicate this true story to my two incredible sons, Darren and Tarek, who helped me through all of our life ordeals and to the Father they never knew…

…and thanks to the universe for the strength and perseverance to get my sons out of a very dangerous and horrifying Civil War in Beirut, Lebanon…

A PLACE I LOVED, AND STILL DO

PROLOGUE

I stood mute and motionless, not a tear running down my face, and watched with horror. The wailing and shrieks grew to a crescendo, and in front of my horrified eyes, his two sisters threw themselves into the gaping hole, clawing their hair from their bloodied roots, as the coffin was lowered into the ground.

CHAPTER ONE

There was no breeze that afternoon. Lying on a chaise looking at the water skiers behind small boats skimming across the lapis blue sea, I could not have imagined being nearer to heaven, but I was wrong. Having tanned my front, I turned over to cook my back.

Simultaneously, our eyes met. Sitting next to me, was the best-looking man I had ever seen in my life. Thick wavy black hair, brown eyes with long eyelashes – and a muscle-bound well-toned tanned body. When he spoke, a tingling sensation of sexual excitement shivered its way up and down my spine.

"Are you German?" he asked in a beguiling accent.

"I'm English" I answered, looking at him admiringly.

As I had been asked this many times before, I was not surprised by the question. He introduced himself and told me his name was Tarek Eddine. What an unusual name, I thought.

"You don't have to call me that", he said shyly. "When I was studying in Fort Worth, Texas, at the International Pilot's School, my American friends called me Terry ... would that be easier?"

"I love the name; it's a crime to change it to anything else. It's very easy to say." I answered.

A few moments later, we swam out to a cluster of rocks about half a mile away from the umbrella-studded shoreline. We scrambled into the slippery rocks and looked back at the skyline.

Beirut is ideally situated between mountains and the sea, and is the home of some of the hardest-working, warmest, and kindest people on earth. During the months of July, August, and September, everyone leaves the city for their mountain homes and villas to escape from the heat. Instead of being rugged or isolated, the mountains around Beirut are the site of flourishing towns, complete with stores, stylish boutiques, elegant restaurants, casinos, and plush nightclubs. Tarek pointed out the famous restaurants literally hanging over the bay, and Pigeon Rock, where he told me that, as a child, he was forbidden by his parents to dive.

I told him that upon our arrival at our Hostel, we found out from Gwen and Pat, our Managers, that the owner of the club in the mountains had scheduled renovations. The Managers of our troupe had given us 3 weeks' vacation. Tarek threw back his head and laughed when I told him that when all the girls heard this announcement, screams of delight had greeted this good news, and Barbara and I had rushed back to our hotel to fetch our bikinis and beach bags for our first swim in the sapphire blue Mediterranean Sea.

"Well it's my lucky day to meet you on your first day of vacation"

We sat for a while looking out at the ocean, and admiring the surrounding views.

2

He looked away quickly, and gazed with obvious deep affection at the wonderful scenery surrounding us.

Being with this good looking man, whom I had only known for perhaps more than an hour, created a combination of sensations within me, which can only be described as animal excitement. Mixed with this, I also felt safe and protected, and an incredible strong feeling of togetherness. It was as though our meeting on the beach had been simply inevitable. The Arabs call it "kismet". I wondered if he felt the same way, or was I under the influence of a too vivid imagination.

We leisurely swim back to Long Beach, and I rejoined my friend, Barbara, who by now was a little more than irritated.

As we stretched out on our towels, he offered me some pure orange juice, and took my left hand shyly ... "I'd like you to meet my family, have something to eat with us, and of course, I'll take you back to your hotel later. Please do accept my invitation."

Looking into his brown velvet eyes, I did not hesitate, I felt completely safe with him.

He proudly told me his family consisted of two brothers, Ali and Achmed, and seven sisters, all of whom lived at home with his parents. There were only a few at home at the moment to meet me, as his parents and the rest of the family were in the mountains. I told Barbara of Tarek's invitation to meet his family.

"You are a fool, Julie" she angrily replied, "You'll end up in one of those harems or worse!"

I understood her being upset – the first day in Beirut, and I had met a gorgeous man.

3

After changing our clothes, we met again a few minutes later at the beach exit. Looking bandbox crisp in a white linen suit, Tarek hailed a cab, and we careered off along the Corniche Mezra, a broad palm tree-lined boulevard that hugged the Mediterranean. As we gazed out of the window, Tarek told me he was a pilot, and was at the moment taking advanced training, and if, and when he passed his last exam, he would be looking for a job.

Abruptly, the car swerved, and we turned into a long alleyway, stopping in front of a large, dreary looking six-story apartment building. It seemed as though there were millions of kids around us, as they ran up to the cab screaming and gawking. Tarek hurriedly whisked me through the front door and up the stone steps. As it was nearly dinnertime, there was a powerful aroma of garlic and onions cooking, and I climbed gingerly upwards, not knowing quite what to expect.

Before he even turned the knob, the door was flung open by a very young, pretty, black-haired girl, about seven years old. Tarek told me this was his youngest sister, Zanab. She looked at me with large wide eyes, and his other two sisters, Kadiche and Emmina, rushed forward to be introduced. They then ran out to the kitchen, and within a few minutes it seemed, large brass trays of fruit and drinks appeared, but I was too keyed up and excited to eat anything.

I noticed Tarek's sisters waited on him deferentially, and treated him like a king, and anything he asked for was immediately produced by one of them. Our conversation flowed easily, and we didn't experience any awkward moments.

Tarek's knowledge of English was not good, but he spoke with an enchanting accent. I tried to converse with his sisters to convey my thanks for their hospitality, and as Tarek translated for me into Arabic, peals of girlish giggles ensued.

We learned more about each other with every passing hour. He was gentle, solicitous and undemanding, with a sharp wit, and a little shy as well. I knew something unusual had happened to me that day. My whole being was fascinated and enthralled by this man. I was experiencing sensations some people, I think, never have the good fortune to feel, feelings I did not want to lose.

When we said good night, standing near the front door of the Hostel, he asked me if we could get together again the next day for lunch and swimming. There was no grabbing, pawing, or forced kisses. I knew I had to see him again for as long as I could, whatever the obstacles.

From that day on, I lived a dream world encompassing only the two of us. We saw each other every day. The days passed quickly, and as each day ended, I realized I was falling madly, passionately in love with this handsome, tempestuous, strong-willed man.

Three weeks to the day, we returned to Long Beach, taking a picnic with us. We swam out to the same cluster of slippery rocks, the scene of our first rendezvous. Intuitively, I knew this was going to be a special day. He shyly asked me to marry him.

Our backgrounds, religion, and heritage were completely opposite, but regardless of all these differences, the barriers seemed miniscule compared to the deep love I felt for him. I realized we were

5

destined to have many problems, frustrations and difficulties, but I was ready to face them, and I didn't care. I flung my arms around his bronzed thick neck, and breathlessly said "Yes, darling, of course I will."

We swam back to the beach. The setting sun threw long shadows over the city, the lights along the bay came on, and dusk brought the day to a close. Tarek suggested returning to his home. His parents and all of his brothers and sisters were away in Harouf in Southern Lebanon, their mountain home, for the weekend.

With his arm around my waist, we ambled slowly down the beach toward the changing cabins; the sand was cool and soft. When we met again a few moments later at the exit, he was wearing cream coloured linen pants, and light beige blazer, with his Body Builders Club insignia embroidered on the breast pocket. As we walked arm in arm to the cab stand - the Saturday night strollers, the open-air cafes, the twinkling lights, the purple and rose quartz sky – resembled a romantic scene from a Cary Grant movie.

Climbing up the stone steps to his apartment, I felt a fluttery feeling of anticipation. Opening the door for me, he told me he would have iced tea, but he had brought some white wine for me, as being Moslem he was not supposed to drink. So we stepped out onto the balcony overlooking the city. The combination of the prayers coming from the nearby Mosque, and the sound of loud Arabic singing drifted up to the balcony, and I tried badly to hum the melody. Tarek smiled and handed me a glass of well-chilled white wine. Gently, we toasted each other and our future life together.

We were alone for the first time in his home. Standing on the dark balcony, with the lights of the city below us, he tenderly pulled me toward him, and we kissed. He took my hand in the semi-darkness, and led me to his bedroom, where the sweet smell of incense enclosed us.

I had waited all my life for this moment. His lovemaking was gentle, sensual and fulfilling. Joy completely overwhelmed me. This was perhaps the real meaning of life ... to be adored by a special person. I felt as though I never wanted him to leave my body. I wanted to share with him everything I had ever experienced in my life before we met ... I wanted to live the rest of my life in his arms...

CHAPTER TWO

My earliest childhood memories in England are hazy. I remember nothing of the war years, and only have a vague memory of hiding under a large oak table in our basement, while screaming German Luftwaffe planes thundered overhead, and finally sirens sounded the "All Clear". My father was somewhere in Egypt and Malaysia fighting the enemy, and my Mother and I were sent from Bristol, a port city, to Falmouth, in Cornwall, for safety.

I remember coming back from school, throwing my clothes on the floor, changing into my swimsuit, and scampering with schoolgirl excitement down to the beach, only minutes away. When I was seven, the first tragedy occurred in my life. My Father, who recently returned from Egypt, told my brother, David and I, that our Mother was very ill. My brother, who was three years older than I said, "What's the matter with Mummy?"

"The doctor hasn't been able to find the cause of her illness, David", Daddy answered in a hesitant tone.

I ran upstairs, and sat down on the top stair outside my Mother's room. I noticed that David was crying silently on the bottom stair, but did not understand why. The doorbell rang, and the doctor hurried upstairs, and went quickly into my mother's room.

It seemed an eternity until the doctor reappeared, and silently walked downstairs, stared at us compassionately. A few moments later, Daddy came downstairs looking tired and drawn.

"I'm afraid your Mother's dead", he said to us.

I looked at David in amazement, as he burst into a fresh outburst of crying.

"What does dead mean?" I asked in all childish innocence.

David looked at me shocked, and bolted out the front door. I wandered aimlessly around the house, still uncomprehending. Little did I realize the impact this would have on my life. At such an early age, I could not foresee how much I would miss my Mother throughout my life. She would never be replaced, and I would never have the special love a mother can give in times of happiness and sadness. She was gone forever.

We were not told anything about our Mother's illness. It wasn't until I was 16 that my Step-Grandmother told me the grim details.

My Father remarried one year later, and my life consisted of being shunted from one relative to another. Birthdays forgotten and broken promises were part of my normal growing up years.

I was sent to a private boarding school in Wiltshire, and David ended up at Sandhurst for military training, so now my Father could spend more time with his new wife. My Stepmother, a beautiful redheaded lady , who was 10 years younger than my Father, was shocked when she discovered her new husband was the father of two children. He had wisely kept this a secret until after the wedding!!

At 12 years of age, my life, I hoped, would really take a turn for the better, when my warm kindly old Grandfather decided to adopt me. He obtained permission from my Father and it was legalized. My own real Grandmother died years before and he had remarried. I really believed now I would have a normal happy home and family life.

It didn't take me long to realize my grandparents were not compatible. They quarrelled and fought constantly, and after an argument, long silences were endured for weeks, each one living in a different part of the house. I couldn't understand why two people would continue to go on living together when they disliked each other so, but later on realized divorce then was still unacceptable and humiliating, so they continued in this living hell.

My Step-Grandmother was irritable and frightening. Her behaviour was unexplainable. I knew she hid a secret bottle, or bottles of cheap wine, burgundy, sherry, or whatever, and throughout the morning would sip on these. I never understood why nothing I ever did pleased her, not understanding at that age the effect the drinking had on her personality.

So many times she was going to leave my Grandfather, and would take me on long desolate walks around the streets of Bristol, complaining, and mentioning putting her head in the oven etc - lovely childhood memories.

I adored my Grandfather. He was tall, grey-haired and very distinguished. He was extremely good to me. He endured the miserable life with her, but was sorry for me, and the hell she put me through.

Three years passed in a maze of confusion and anxiety. I blossomed into a teenager, and that summer, I visited my Auntie Phyllis, who owned a cafe and bed and breakfast resort in St. Austell, Cornwall, overlooking a pebbly beach. My 15th birthday was approaching, an exciting day for most girls. After a hard long day in the cafe, Auntie Phyllis baked a large cake with fifteen candles, and produced lots of gifts. Everyone sang "Happy Birthday", and we sat down to munch on the delicious cake.

The shrilling tone of the telephone interrupted our party, and Auntie picked it up. She listened intently, and looked up, tense and pale.

"What is it?" Anne, my cousin and I asked simultaneously. Ignoring us, she listened some more and then said:

"Thank you, we'll be there."

She looked white and drawn, and said in a quiet, shocked voice:

"It's Dad, he's dead."

I looked at her aghast – my whole world crumbling around me, my Grandfather dead, I could not believe it.

"How did it happen?" Anne asked.

"He just dropped dead in the driveway, while he was repairing his car."

I was shaking inside. My poor Grandfather, but at least the only consolation was he did not suffer.

After the funeral, I was aware I could not stay on in the house much longer with my Step-Grandmother, as I knew she would become even more impossible to

11

live with. I planned to leave as soon as it was legal to do so.

Great memories and times spent together with my Grandfather were flashing through my mind. He had owned a typically English sweetshop in Bristol, and my happiest memories are of visiting him after school in his little office in the back. He would be sitting in his favourite chair, working on paperwork. He would fetch ice cream for me, and then ask about my school work for the evening. He was a stickler about my doing my homework, and would sit with me each night until I had finished.

No TV, going out or playing with friends was allowed to disturb my assignment for the evening. He had been so good and kind to me and the only stable person left. Again, there was a deep void in my life.

The time for me to move on was imminent. But where and how?

I returned to the only home I knew. My Step-Grandmother sold the house in Fishponds a few months later, and brought a four-story apartment building in Clifton.

Before he died, my Grandfather kept suggesting I enrol for secretarial training, so I would always be able to support myself under any circumstances. I enrolled in Clark's Secretarial College, as he would have wished, and pushed myself to learn Shorthand, typing, and many other office procedures. I hated the idea but there was no choice, and spent two years getting my business training.

One day in early June, my Step-Grandmother called me into her room:

"I have something unpleasant to tell you."

I knew basically what it might be but asked casually, "What is it?"

"Well, I've been obligated to tell you the true story of your Mother's death." I looked at her. I didn't really want to know, but nothing would stop her now.

"It's not a pleasant story. Your Mother was pregnant again, and didn't want another child."

"Why not?" I innocently enquired.

"Julie dear", she said patiently, "Your Father was a 'ladies man' and she was afraid if she delivered another child, she would become fat and unappealing, and your Father would start looking around for another conquest, so she decided to try to do something about it."

"So what killed her?" I asked in dismay.

"She tried to get rid of the child, and in doing so, killed herself, I'm afraid" she replied. "A little knowledge is a dangerous thing."

The few short fond memories of my Mother passed through my mind. To think she died so young and so needlessly. If the unwanted pregnancy had occurred today, she would be alive and well. My Mother lived too early to be saved.

Innocent dates with various young men, holding hands, kissing in the moonlight on the beach in Weston Super Mare were fun, but having to rush back knowing my Step-Grandmother was waiting and watching for me was a nightmare. I had no idea about sex, and thought if I did more than hold hands, I would get pregnant, nobody talked about sex and the only things I heard were from girlfriends sniggering and whispering about it, I was completely ignorant. My first boyfriend, Ivan (you never forget that) got serious and invited me to meet his family. I got so scared, I knew I had to leave Bristol, the time had come to run away. There was more to life than marriage and children, I was sure.

I had been working at the Bristol Evening World, had completed and graduated from the secretarial college, and was paying my Grandmother every week for my keep plus polishing the floors, and most of the housework but I wanted to live, live, live!!! See the world, travel, learn a foreign language, see, smell, touch, feel ... Taking my own future in my hands, at the sweet virginal age of 17, I was ready to take my first shaky step up the thrilling and scary ladder of life.

CHAPTER THREE

I left Bristol and my Step-Grandmother with pleasure, and went to Temple Meads for my train journey to London. It was a new and exhilarating feeling stepping off the train in London, not knowing anyone, or where to stay, an experience, little did I know I would repeat many times throughout my life. London was enormous and frightening compared to Bristol, and as I stepped onto the platform at Paddington, I looked around with apprehension.

I thought the safest and most reliable place to stay would be the YWCA. I found my way there through the teaming masses.

Taking the underground, jostling amid the rush, bustle and excitement of the big town was thrilling. My next objective was to obtain a job, which was not hard, as I now had secretarial training. My real ambition was to become a model, so I also enrolled in the Cherry Marshall School of Modelling, and started immediately taking classes in the evenings, and working during the day.

Still being a virgin, I was confused and curious by the excited chatter of the girls discussing various sexual activities, when we gathered together in the evenings, in the YWCA lounge. I felt left out, unwomanly, and ignorant, and could not offer any information to the conversation. One evening, I made a decision to change this, and went out with the sole intention of losing my virginity.

It was, of course, as I deserved – unexciting, painful, and unpleasant. I hoped, one day, to have real feelings, accompanying a wonderful relationship, love, romance, and a feeling even Khalil Gibran found difficult to describe.

My training over, I found a job as a fashion model on Oxford Street, and spent many feet-aching hours modelling summer, autumn and winter clothes. Standing motionless, while pins were stuck in the material on my body, seemed a somewhat dull ending to my dreams.

In the meantime, I moved out of the YWCA, and was sharing a flat with two other girls in Kensington. All of us, intent on studying, fighting off would-be lovers, being closeted up like oysters on the underground, and strap hanging - were now part of my world.

The gutsy feeling of London was exciting to me, and the lurid back streets and nightclubs of Soho were fascinating. I saw many tourists in the strip joints and bars in the area, and was envious of the money these girls were making, but could I take my clothes off? I enjoyed putting them on. The clothes in London were fabulous, and very difficult for me to ignore. Every week, my entire pay check would be spent on clothes. Who cared about saving at my age?

Two years seemed to pass too fast, and again, the restless urge to travel swept over me. I knew I wanted to see the world and let someone else pay for my wanderlust.. that was it ... but how?

Entering beauty contests for fun and money had given me confidence to be on stage in front of a lot of people, in high heels and a swimsuit, and I had won a little cash. It was amazing to me to see some of the girls' intensity in the contests, and their mothers' irate anger when their particular little darling lost. The fights and chaos in the dressing rooms was something to behold.

One day, completely by accident, I was looking through a local magazine entitled "Show Biz" ...and there it was, an advertisement for a show touring Europe who needed Showgirls, dancers and singers. Being cheeky and full of audacity and verve, I decided to apply. I had no experience in dancing or show business, but what the hell! ... Nothing ventured, nothing gained!

The rehearsal hall was difficult to find, and it was a frustrating few hours before I found the big brown building and the studio mentioned in the advertisement. I pushed opened the door and looked around, and found many young attractive girls standing about talking to a middle-aged lady. She walked up to me.

"Are you auditioning as a Showgirl or a dancer?"

"I think a Showgirl" I answered.

"Well, what experience do you have?" she asked sweetly, looking me up and down intently.

"None, I'm afraid", not knowing where to look.

"Well, can you sing at all?" she asked impatiently.

"Yes, I can", I replied, clutching at what I thought was my last chance.   I did know how to sing, but never received any professional training.

"Well, take this microphone and let's hear you", she demanded.

I quickly thought of a nice ballad of Marilyn Monroe's entitled "I've Never Been Loved Before" from "Some Like it Hot", took the microphone and began to sing.   I stood nervously waiting as she walked over to see me.

"You did very well. You are hired. Can you be ready to leave for Brussels, Belgium next Friday for a month of intensive rehearsals?"

I looked at her incredulously.   After further explanations and discussions of the contract, money, countries, etc., it began to sink in that I was really on my way. How I had done it, I had no idea ... but I was going somewhere ... at this stage, I really didn't care where!

Gwen Lane and Pat Wallis, the owners, told me they had a signed contract for Brussels first, then Norway, and perhaps Sweden. I sauntered over and introduced myself to the other showgirls Linda, Jean and Barbara – all their names getting mixed up in my mind.

In a robot kind of condition, I returned in a state of euphoria to my apartment. Running up the many tedious stairs, I burst into the flat screaming out the good news to my flat mates. Making arrangements and frantic phone calls took up the rest of that evening, and I knew sleep would be impossible, until the following Friday of my departure. It came at last, and as I travelled to Paddington Station, I kept pinching myself that I was really leaving. Meeting at the pre-arranged rendezvous, I joined a fever-pitched group of girls, also very anxious to be on their way.

The tedious long journey with many train changing, and one ferry boat ride, created a close band of comradeship within the group, consisting of about 15 girls. Gwen told me a young French singer would be joining us in Brussels, and he would be the only male ... poor guy! Chatting with the other girls, I found out most of them were well experienced in other shows, but they re-assured me Pat and Gwen would teach me well, and I would soon learn all the routines.

At last we arrived at the historic old town of Brussels. Frantic screaming girls running around, lost suitcases and misplaced tickets all settled, we all began pairing off at the hotel for our various rooms. Linda, a tall good-looking redhead attached herself to me, and in a friendly gesture, suggested we room together.

"Is that alright with you, Julie?"

"Of course Linda, that's fine." I answered.

We soon located our room, and set about unpacking and settling in. Our shared fears and concern about the long and arduous rehearsals ahead of us were discussed, and then the long tiring journey took its toll, and we both decided to turn in.

Just as I was ready to jump into bed, Linda walked over to me and sat down.

"Julie, have you ever had sex with a woman?" she asked, looking at me challengingly.

I looked at her in amazement. My education in all fields of sex had been little, but this was a completely closed book. She edged closer, as if she was going to kiss me.

"Well, have you?"

Backing away and sitting up sharply, I replied.

"No, Linda, I haven't. Why?"

I was extremely nervous by this time, but was trying unsuccessfully to appear cool and nonchalant.

"Well, you should try it, it's much better than men, and no complications!"

That was it; I threw off the blankets, and ran as far away from her as possible, without leaving the room.

"I'm quite content with men at the moment, and don't want to try anything new, so forget it!"

She looked at me in complete disgust, and began sauntering back to her own bed, sarcastically remarking what a square I was. Swaying her hips, she suddenly turned and provocatively slipped her bra off. Seductively moving her fingers over her entire body, she looked at me teasingly and whispered...

"Wouldn`t you enjoy experiencing and enjoying my body like this?"

I shook my head and walked into the bathroom, and locked it, amid screams of laughter from Linda.

"Scaredy Cat, that's what you are", she screamed from the bedroom.

Tossing and turning the whole night, sleeping little, I knew I would have to request a re-assigned room first thing in the morning.

Meeting for breakfast the next day, bright and early, we found out we could walk to the "Moulin Rouge" where we would be performing, it was so close. The first day's rehearsal was gruelling and that's all we did every day – rehearse, rehearse, rehearse.

Pat and Gwen showed us some mock-ups of the posters which would be distributed, and pointed to the name of the show – "Las Vegas". Glancing at one, I noticed my name, coupled with Pierre's, as the opening singers, and I was nervous and thrilled to death to see my name on a poster, wow!

She gave me the song sheet for the opening number "New York, New York", and told me to learn the words by next rehearsal. Pointing out a slim, dark-haired young man chatting with the orchestra, she said

"Julie, that's Pierre. I want you to start practicing with him, as I need to see how your voices blend together."

I looked nervously at Pierre, and hoped we would sound good together. Going through all the steps and routines in my mind was confusing, and it seemed too much to learn, and this was only the first week! Chatting with the girls in the dressing room, we counted up our changes, throughout the show, from head-dresses to shoes, which consisted of 10. The timing was vital, and each change was executed to the second, for our next cued entrance.

The following weeks were spent in non-stop rehearsals. We awoke, walked to rehearsals, ate a little, returning again to rehearsal, and later fell exhausted into bed. This continued for three weeks. We could not have any social life, and by this time, really nobody cared what city we were in, or how Brussels looked, and were all too tired to care.

The costumes, personally designed by Pat and Gwen, were delivered at last for our final dress rehearsal. They were breathtaking. The sequinned head-dresses and expensive silk and satin materials looked and felt luxurious and glamorous, and I delicately stepped into them for the first time.

Carefully applying my stage makeup, and fixing my hair, I nervously repeated the words of the song over and over in my mind, and tried to recall all the positions. A knock sounded on the dressing room door. I walked to the wings, my mind a blank – what would I do? I stepped into the stage into the footlights with Pierre close by, and began to sing. Suddenly my memory and voice returned as if my magic, and standing next to Pierre I smiled, when I noticed I towered above him in my high heels and tall head-dress.

The final scene unfolded, and our finale completed, we all ran back to our dressing rooms, to await the final verdict from Pat and Gwen on our performance. They both appeared at the door, smiling broadly.

"Well, girls, it was fantastic! You now have our permission to leave the club and see Brussels and have a good time."

Whoops of joy greeted this announcement, and we ran out into the night to discover the town.

The "Moulin Rouge" nightclub was impressive. A spiralling red-carpeted staircase, glittering chandeliers above, led into revolving glass doors. Inside, sexy intimate lighting shone onto small cozy tables, mirrors surrounding the whole room. Centred was a magnificent large stage, hung with heavy velvet brocade curtains, securely closed by ornate gold leaved clasps. Outside the front, and on the walls, large posters advertising the upcoming event were displayed, and Ralph Cleassa, the owner of the club and Pat and Gwen were anxious for a large crowd on opening night.

The long awaited opening gala night arrived...

The club was packed. I tiptoed onto the stage and discreetly peeked through the curtains to check the crowd out, then ran back to the dressing room. A last minute frantic look at my make-up and hair, and then the orchestra began its overture. Joining Pierre in the wings, we walked onstage together for our opening number. The one and a half hours flew by at a frantic pace; rushing back and forth between changes, and then the finale music was heard. Smiling broadly, we took our bows amid thunderous applause. Panting and breathless we all went to our various dressing rooms, and flopped exhausted into our chairs. The show was a success.

Now we had all earned some relaxation and fun. The following day, Janet, Carol and I toured Brussels' quaint old streets and buildings, and visited the famous monuments and statues. Each day we roamed around a little more, and stared fascinated at the infamous "Peeing Boy". Walking around the 'Red Light' district, we peered through the windows at the ladies of the night on display, and tried to catch glimpses of other shows and acts in town. The three months passed by quickly and our final closing night arrived. Pat told me the next evening a completely new troupe was opening. She explained it was an all male troupe of "female impersonators" and certainly might be worth watching.

Janet, Carol, Jeannie, Maureen, and I decided to make an evening of it, and booked a table as close as possible to the large stage. We all sat eyes wide open throughout the entire show. Their finale featuring an exotic looking redhead, stripping to lilting music, languishing on a red velvet couch, somehow endowed with voluptuous bosoms, had us all shaking our heads in wonderment.

"I've never seen a woman do a better strip-tease than that", I said turning to the girls. Turning around, I saw every eye staring at the tall red-headed star, originally male, walk in. I knew we were all thinking the same thing.

"Which restroom would the star enter?"

Laughing gaily, clad in a skin-tight black evening dress with deep decollate, he/she pushed open the ladies' room door and slammed it shut. Well, that was that.

We all pushed our chairs back, and arm in arm, walked up the staircase into the cool night air.

CHAPTER FOUR

Our contract finished, the next day we were leaving Brussels for Antwerp – "the diamond centre", our next assignment. This was a unique French-like town, full of small sidewalk cafes, and bubbling friendly people. The show was well received, and again the three months was completed, and we were all again trooping back to the railway station.

We chugged out of Antwerp station, and as the hours passed by, watched through the carriage window fascinated by the changing scenery and different countries crossed. Travelling through Switzerland and Austria, on each country's border, a guard would enter the compartment, check our passports and add another visa. After many hours of absorbing sights and sounds, and hours of endless laughter and giggles, we glimpsed our first sight of the outskirts of Oslo, Norway.

Oslo, famous for its dangerously high sloping ski mountains and sandy beaches, was not disappointing. Settling into our small, clean Pension, Pat and Gwen picked us up to check out our new nightclub. Walking in, I realized it was the largest we had ever entertained in, and adjacent to the main club was an after-hours restaurant for late night dancing, which stayed open until 4 a.m. Jeannie, Maureen and I ran onto the stage, and looked out over the ballroom to the 3 and 4 tiered balconies surrounding us. I was really tired after the long train journey, and so were the rest of the girls, so we left the club and returned back to our Pension for an early night's sleep, so we could be ready for rehearsal the next morning.

Gwen gathered us all together, and then stepped on the stage for her usual opening remarks. Hesitating a little, she continued.

"There is going to be a little change in the show here, as the owner is demanding one of you perform some kind of a strip-tease." We started at each other. What was this? Gwen went on.

"They told me they have hired a juggling act and a comedienne, to give you girls time to change between sets, but as far as the strip-tease goes, I will first ask one of you to volunteer, otherwise I will have to nominate someone to do this. I'm sorry, my hands are tied."

She walked dejectedly to her seat. I knew, as did everyone else, nobody would volunteer for it, and she would have to order someone. She walked slowly back up the stairs to the stage.

"Well, it's obvious I will have to make this decision, so I am going to ask Linda and Julie to rehearse something for me. I will put the choreography together, and then I will choose the best of the two."

Glancing at Linda, I could see she was furious, and wore a look of complete disgust on her face. Gwen beckoned us both over, and began to discuss various routines, and songs we could sing, while

26

performing. Linda sharply reminded her she could not sing, and calling Pat to her side, made alternative choreography suggestions for her. The next couple of days, Linda and I practiced our different acts. Nervously checking with Pat and Gwen on the acceptable boundaries, she informed me we stripped down to large pasties and a very brief bikini. An enveloping silk cape was thrown around our shoulders, as we took our final bow I decided to sing my original audition number, and at the final rehearsal, Linda and I were literally quaking in our shoes. After our performances, Pat and Gwen congratulated us both, but told me my act was more suitable for this type of show.

Amidst confusion and opening night nerves, "Las Vegas" opened, and the crowd roared with approval. I was flattered and surprised when roses and champagne began arriving nightly in my dressing room. Invitations accompanied these gifts, and I received personally escorted trips to all the scenic sights, restaurants in the hills and yacht parties. One evening, I was introduced by the owner, Olaf Berge, to meet a blond, blue-eyed attractive man, who introduced himself as Lars Schmidt. He took, me to many exciting spots around Oslo, and knew from my conversation my 21st birthday was in a few days. He casually suggested asking Pat and Gwen for the night off, so he could fly me to Stockholm for the evening. We could celebrate there, and return the following day in time for my performance.

Dressed in a comfortable pants suit and carrying my overnight bag, Lars picked me up from the pension. A silver-blue Cessna was waiting at the airport, gassed up and ready to take flight. It looked terribly small to me, and I approached nervously.

"Lars, are you really going to fly this thing?" He laughed heartedly.

"I fly it all the time, Julie. It's really quite safe, don't worry."

I loved flying, but preferred a plane you could at least walk about in, and hoped my stomach could handle what I was sure would be a bumpy ride. The flight was peaceful and tranquil; however, peering from the cockpit, I watched fascinated as the white clouds swirled madly around. Suddenly, without any warning, we descended from the clouds into the clear blue sky, and he excitedly pointed out below the first signs of Stockholm. We started to slowly descend to the distant airport, and I looked enquiringly around at the high-rises, and the outline of the clean sparkling city.

Stepping carefully from the plane, we walked hand in hand, digesting all the sights and sounds, and he later took me to his favourite French restaurant for dinner. Romantic violin players serenaded us in the background, while foundations of water cascaded above, and brilliant shimmering lights danced off the water. The sight-seeing was over too soon, and we slowly returned to our little cosy hotel for the evening. Lars was a passionate and considerate lover and the night was unfortunately soon over.

Flying back the next day, now enjoying every moment of the flight, he dropped me at the club just in the nick of time for the opening number. It was now back to work, and my 21st birthday was a memory.

Even though it was August, Oslo was not very warm and chatting with other Norwegians, I found out you needed to buy two completely different closets of clothes if you lived there, one for the very hard winter, and one for the summer. Long-johns and heavy winter coats were a must to keep out the tremendous cold, so they told me. I was sure glad we were there in the summer, and not the winter.

The contract was again coming to a close, and feeling sad, I kissed Lars fondly, and waved frantically to him until he was out of sight.

Feeling deflated and very tired after our long journey, we steamed into Paddington Station. Saying tearful goodbyes to all the girls in the troupe, each one a special friend, but now all of us going our separate ways. I aimlessly caught the underground to my old flat, still occupied by my two roommates.

London seemed colder, bleaker and more alien to me after my adventures, and even the seedy scent of Soho could not turn me around. The days seemed long, and the nights longer, and even with my two friends running around the flat, I could not cheer up. I was now a night person, but to exist I needed to reverse, and become a day person. I started on the dull routine of doing temporary secretarial jobs until, I hoped, a new contract would materialize for Pat and Gwen.

The days and weeks went slowly by, and I again longed for more blue skies and sandy beaches. I had an offer from the Follies Bergere in Paris, as some poor English girl had been shot on the street there, but knowing it was "no clothing at all", and my Grandmother very heavily frowned on it, declined it.

The long awaited telephone call came at last from Pat and Gwen and told me they had just signed a new contract for Italy and the Middle East. Ecstatic was not the word, and checking on the contract conditions, I asked her when we would be leaving. She told me departure date was in one week, and our meeting place was under the same clock as before, at Paddington Station.

"Will we be learning any new routines?" I asked.

"Well, it's possible you will have to learn belly dancing, as we will need to have one Middle Eastern number in the show. Do you think you can dance without shoes, because that's the way it's done?"

"Sure, sounds like fun to me", I replied.

Slamming the phone down and screaming out the good news to my roommates, I spent the rest of the evening calling all my relatives and other friends to tell them of my next travels.

The next few days passed slowly, but at least it was time to re-pack my clothes for the trip. Feeling just as excited as the first time, I looked around for the group. Pat and Gwen saw me first, and waving anxiously, beckoned me over and introduced me around to the new troupe.

The long journey to Italy began. Chatting with the new girls, I found out there was only Carol, Janet and I left from the old group. Reacquainting ourselves again, we reminisced and joked about the ups and downs of our last tour, and the variety of interesting people met so far. And our next journey started.

Genoa, we found, was a bustling large seaport town, full of surprises and pinches. We loved the

Italian food, bad for our figures, and the over-zealous men. The beaches and scenery were beautiful, and one day, Carol, Janet and I decided to visit Portofino. Shading my eyes, I looked out over the picturesque bay at the rainbow colours of the sailboats, and green/blue sea, and vividly recalled the song of nostalgia dedicated to its name. The song aptly described the unsurpassed beauty around me.

We opened to packed houses in Genoa, and then went on to Torino and Tirrenia, white-sanded seaside resorts, great places for sunbathing and sightseeing.

The day arrived at last for our return scheduled journey to Genoa, and our journey up the gangplank, to board our luxury cruise ship for our long trip to Egypt.

The liner "Prince Valiant" was not prepared for 15 crazy showgirls and dancers and we literally turned the ship upside down. We scampered around, causing havoc in our bikinis, and spent most of our days sunbathing and swimming in the large pool. We danced romantically in the moonlight, flirted madly, and were all given personally escorted tours of the engine room by the Captain.

Looking over the railings at the water's many changing colors, and inhaling the different scents of the sea, I felt so content and tranquil, and a hazy glow of contentment washed over me, as I felt at one with sea and nature.

After seven days of fun and sun, tensions mounting, we approached the port city of Alexandria, Egypt...

CHAPTER FIVE

As we stepped off the boat, an engulfing, stifling heat, rushing people and foreign-sounding voices filled the air. A little apprehensive and tense, we were all chauffeured from Alexandria to Cairo in Mercedes taxis, and peering out of the window, we were surprised at the contrasts from picturesque buildings to run-down alleys and bazaars. Honking horns, screeching traffic and tires, traffic lights ignored, shouting and gesturing in Arabic and complete chaos, created the atmosphere of Cairo. Thankfully, in one piece, we drove up to our hotel.

That evening, we met in the lobby of the hotel, and picking up two or three service taxis, drove over to the "Casino Fontana" to look over the nightclub where we were scheduled to appear. This was formerly the palace of ex-King Farouk and it had a regal and majestic appearance appropriate for a King. Walking into the massive courtyard, marble and stone statues decorated the entrance. Stepping into the club, we looked through the windows to the landscaped garden, and with awe, glimpsed the River Nile flowing smoothly by, all of which gave it the appearance of a religious sanctuary.

Our first night was again filled with tension. We now performed our belly dancing well, and the costumes were sensuous, yet classically elegant. The audience applauded loudly at our final scene, but a special ovation greeted our combined belly dancing number. As we were all dressing to leave to return to our hotel, Pat Suddenly appeared in our dressing rooms.

"Girls, wait a second. I have something to tell you. Sit down all of you." The chattering abruptly came to a halt, and we all sat down.

"I have just been told by the owner, Mustapha Hijawi, that he expects you girls to sit at the tables and entertain his clients."

We all looked at each other, aghast. What next?

"I'm sorry", she said, "Nothing was in my contract, but I think if we all look out for each other and insist on leaving together each evening, we might be able to stick it out."

Poor Pat was nearly in tears, as she felt she had been taken advantage of, and her artistic talents were tarnished. She rushed from the dressing room, and left us in stunned silence.

"Well, it seems we don't have much choice", I said.

"Doesn't look like it", Carol said. "Unless you all feel like hitching it back to England."

We all nervously laughed, and forcing a smile, realized we were stuck.

CHAPTER SIX

So night after night, our final curtain call completed, we all changed and returned to the club to sit, dance and drink with the rich Egyptians who crowded into the club.

Most of the girls started to enjoy themselves, dining and dancing, and every day became more familiar with the customs and mentality of the country we were visiting. The Egyptians were always polite and gentlemanly, only too proud to discuss all the interesting and colourful areas of the region we should visit.

Tired of the superficial charade of nightclubs and expensive hotels, one evening before going to the club, I decided to venture out on my own. Borrowing a yasmack from one of the hotel employees, hiding my blond hair beneath the hood, and slipping on flat local shoes, I furtively ran into the street, unobserved. Walking at a steady pace, I looked around back alleys, checked on out-of-the-way authentic Egyptian sidewalk cafes, and walked around curio shops and souks. I felt no fear, as the law of the land was so strict, I felt safe. I was distressed at the amount of beggars on the streets, and the contracts between rich and poor, living so close, but yet worlds apart.

One of the regular customers of the "Casino Fontana", Omar Idris, had graciously invited Carol and me to visit The Sphinx and Pyramids the next day. His chauffeured-driven car arrived to pick us up, and we sank down comfortably on the drive towards the desert. The day was cool, but the sun overhead was blue and cloudless. We drove up to the "Semiramis Hotel", whose balconies overlooked the Pyramids. We sat down, and gazed out over the Sahara desert. Omar suggested hiring Arabic horses for our short ride to the Pyramids, and walked off to make the arrangements. A young handsome white-turbaned attendant helped us both onto the handsome animals, and we cantered leisurely towards the Pyramids. We all slowly climbed the many stone and musty steps to the top, and marvelled at the skill and gruelling hard work taken to build such an historic monument.

Leisurely trotting back to the "Seminiramis", Omar ordered lunch, and we all sat down in the courtyard looking out at the ancient structures and beauty of our surroundings. A large mezza appeared, and to complement this, their local liquor, "Arak", was brought to the table. Carol and I had never tasted anything like this before, but it complemented so well the variety of fresh and interesting dishes laid out before us. Sipping it for the first time, I made a gruesome face. It tasted like aniseed, but after a couple of drinks, it began to taste good.

Chatting over lunch, Omar excitedly told us about a mysterious nightclub in the desert named "Sahara City". His eyes sparkling, he went on to describe the massive luxurious flowing white silk tent, where inside belly dancers swayed, and exotically dressed waters served you wine in long silver goblets, while guests relaxed on velvet cushions.

He invited us to go with him the following Saturday after the show. As a regular patron of the club, he knew he could get us both off after the show for the evening. He checked with Mustapha Hijawi, the owner, and we waited anxiously for the outing.

"What should I wear, Omar?" I asked. "If I have to ride on a horse to get to the club, I suppose it should be some sort of pantsuit."

"Yes, I would say so", he smiled mischievously, "Unless you want to ride side-saddle, like the British."

Omar was an olive-complexioned, very good looking man in his early 30's, and seemed to exude good breeding and sensitivity. Carol and I felt completely at ease with him, and enjoyed his company. I decided to wear a beautiful pant suit in shocking pink, and Carol also chose dressy evening pants and a sequined top. We couldn't wait for our last final bow of the evening, and ran back into the dressing room to change. Outside, Omar waited in his limousine, smiled his teasing smile, and patted the comfortable seat.

"I don't see how a man can be so lucky", he said "to have two such beautiful women with him."

"We're the lucky ones, Omar", I replied "to have such a wonderful host and gentlemen to show us the best of Egypt."

He acknowledged my compliment with a stronger clasp of my hand, and shouted to the driver to get a move on.

The twinkling lights of Cairo, the incessant honking of cars, and general hubbub of the city soon was left behind, and we drove up again to the Hotel for our ride to the club. Two arrogant Arab horses were brought to us, and Carol and I swung up like veterans, and rode off into the desert, more like Bedouins than Limeys ...

After about twenty minutes of riding in the arid moonlight desert, we essentially made out some lights and could hear some sounds of lilting Arabic music – we had arrived at Sahara City. Omar, looking extremely dashing in English-type jodhpurs, a silk shirt, and silver riding crop, led the way around to the rear where many horses and camels were tethered.

"Well, we're here", he shouted.

"Lila!" he shouted, clapping his hands for attention.

A few moments later, a beautiful black-haired voluptuous girl in a brightly coloured belly dancing outfit appeared from the voluminous tent. He ran towards her, talking rapidly in Arabic, and then gaily beckoned us over.

Gazing down at her with intensive admiration and desire, he pulled her towards us.

"I want to introduce you to the best belly dancer in the Middle East." Lila looked at us in surprise. More Arabic ensued, and then after a little while, she burst into a smile.

"How nice to meet you, I hear you also do belly dancing." We both laughed.

"Nothing like yours, I'm afraid", Carol replied.

"Actually, Lila, it's only one number in the whole show", I added.

"Well its better than none at all" she laughingly replied.

"Let's all go inside, and I will perform a special number of all of you, especially Omar", she looked seductively in his direction. Carol and I exchanged glances, realizing they must be more than friends.

Bowing, turban-headed waiters ushered us in, and we were escorted to a corner and sat down with pleasure on a velvet couch covered with many silk and satin pillows. Goblets of wine and food appeared as if by magic, and we both just stared about us in awe. Scenes from "Arabian Nights" floated through my head, and the haunting belly dancing music grew now to a crescendo, as Lila danced onto the neon lit stage.

Her costume was tantalizing, and her dancing was mesmerizing, with hips swaying, she danced over to our table, and dragged Omar to his feet onto the stage. Obviously having danced with Lila before, they complimented each other and together created a sensuous rhythmic couple.

Carol and I were lost in the sights and sounds around us, so were startled on hearing a deep masculine voice addressing us.

"Are you guests of Omar?" he asked.

"Why, yes we are", I replied.

He was a small grey-haired distinguished elderly, well-dressed gentleman, with twinkling brown eyes.

"Let me introduce myself. I am Rashid Bakier, owner of the club. I bid you welcome. How lucky Omar is to have such lovely company. May I join you and wait for Omar?"

"But of course", I replied, turning back to look again at the stage.

Omar suddenly appeared at the table and sat down, as Lila's music accelerated to her finale. Now on her knees, stretching her head and arms far back over her head, her whole body vibrating, the music raced. She got to her feet and began twirling in circles, and as the music came to a thunderous halt, took her final bows, amid boisterous shouts of approval.

After a few moments of polite conversation, Lila reappeared dressed now in a red cocktail outfit, and sat down next to Rashid. Dancing close to Omar under the canopy humming the lilting music, I knew the evening would have to come to a close, but I didn`t want it to ever end. Around 4 a.m., the last flap was fastened on the tent, and it was time to put my foot into the stirrups once more for our ride back to the hotel.

Cantering back was breathtaking, as the sunrise loomed overhead, and the eerie silence surrounding us was mystical. The white sand was all around us, and seemed to never end, and I felt as an alien lost in the sea of sand. After a peaceful ride to our hotel, and clasping Omar`s hand in thanks for the wonderful evening, we sped upstairs for a sound and peaceful sleep.

A couple of nights later, Omar suggested we join a party of friends on a romantic ferry boat trip down the Nile. Carol was busy, but I accepted with thanks. He said food and wine would be served on board, and hubble bubble pipes would be passed around, if I wanted to try one. Asking who were the other friends, he told me Rashid and Lila were going to be one of the couples accompanying us.

"Rashid and Lila?" I queried.

"Oh, didn't you know, Julie? Rashid is Lila's husband."

The shocked look on my face surprised him.

"Why are you shocked? I thought you knew that."

"Actually, Omar, I thought you two had something going, and well, he is so much older than her."

A slight pause and change of tone told me everything.

"Well, that's the way it is, I'm afraid", his voice now cold and distant.

"I'll be looking forward to Tuesday night, and will pick you up at 11:30 p.m. after your show. Goodbye" and he stalked out.

Chatting it over with Carol in the dressing room later, fixing our make-up, we were both confused by the situation. I concluded it must be one of those pre-arranged marriages, and given the opportunity, I sure intended to find out.

Tuesday night at 11:30 p.m., there was Omar, waiting in his limousine, looking bright-eyed and happy, obviously looking forward to a wonderful evening. I greeted Rashid and Lila and the other couple warmly, and stepping carefully onto the ferry, we gracefully glided down the famous River Nile. Omar gaily passed around the bubble pipe, and after a few tentative smokes, I began to experience a euphoric relaxed feeling. Arak and local dishes were shared around, and I watched the unusual scenery passing by. A couple of hours of delightful conversation ensued, and the smooth voyage continued. Even now in my hazy condition, I kept catching Omar giving quick secretive glances to Lila, which were returned with loving, longing looks of pent-up desire. Rashid sat complacently, looking out to sea, not appearing to notice anything unusual going on between them. Stepping out of the boat at the dockside of "The Casino Fontana", I stumbled a little. Omar and Rashid gallantly ran to support me from either side.

"Are you alright, Julie?" Omar asked, as I began to stumble even more.

"Well, I do feel kind of dizzy and funny. I don't know how to explain it", I said, Feeling like a child who had mixed her drinks.

Rashid laughed. "Well, Hashish does have that effect on someone not used to it."

"What?!!" I exclaimed, shocked. "I didn't know it was Hashish!"

"Oh yes, we smoke it all the time, but you are not used to it", laughed Omar.

Clapping his hands again for service, Omar barked out an order for immediate strong black local coffee, and as I sipped it scalding hot, my head began to clear. Saying my goodbyes to Rashid, Lila, and their friends, Omar drove me back to my hotel.

He kissed my hand, and walked me dutifully to the lift. walking slowly, I thankfully dropped onto my bed as waves of nausea swept over me and then passed ... what a night! I fell immediately into a deep sound sleep.

CHAPTER SEVEN

The following week, Omar again took Carol and I on a trip to Luxor, and we spent a sun-drenched day watching archaeologists excavating and digging for new tombs and treasures, and walked around fascinated by the ancient structures and sights.

The three months once again was coming to a close, and all the troupe was thrilled to be going to Beirut. Wonderful stories were told to us about Beirut, Lebanon – the beaches, the nightclubs, and good-looking friendly people. We were anxious to find out for ourselves if all this was true.

The closing night of our show, Rashid, Lila and Omar booked a table at the club to watch our last farewell performance. As the show finished, I ran back to change, and then noticed a commotion going on around Omar's table. Waiters were rushing crazily around, shouting and gesturing, and I paled as I saw a prone body being taken out of the club on a stretcher. Asking around, I found out from the owner that Rashid had suffered a slight heart attack and had been rushed to the hospital.

Carol and I waited anxiously for news, and at last, Omar called to say he was out of danger. The next day was our last in Cairo, and I was extremely curious to receive some answers to a lot of questions that were intriguing me. Before he hung up, I reminded him we were leaving the next day, and could he come by the hotel for lunch and a chat.

"Of course, I intended to, I will miss you, but you never know where we will meet again or when."

I was not sure whether he would open up to me as to his true feelings for Lila, and why she was married to such an older man as Rashid. He walked into the hotel, looking gaunt and drawn. Settling down to a large salad, I tentatively opened up the subject. After a little prompting, he began to tell his story.

"Julie, Lila and I were born in the same village outside Cairo, and grew up together. We became sweethearts, and loved each other desperately. One day, she left the village to visit Cairo, and her relatives there arranged a meeting between her and Rashid." He paused a second, obviously in pain.

"It was love at first sight for Rashid, and being from a well-known prominent family in the city, Lila was forced to marry him against her own wishes. That's it, Julie."

With tears in his eyes, he went on to say he was still suffering, but other than kidnapping her, and leaving the country, his hands were tied.

"I do hope you and Carol didn't mind being part of the group with Lila, as this is the only way I could be close to her and in her company without attracting suspicion."

I nodded. I had suspected this right from the beginning.

"I do want to thank you, Omar, for giving us such a wonderful stay in Cairo. I know I will never forget it."

Hugging him tightly, I told him I hoped one day he would be able to declare his love for Lila, and they could be as one together.

The trip to Beirut we found out from Pat and Gwen was going to be in a bus.....a bus???....We looked aghast at Pat and Gwen when she said we were going to go part of the way to Baghdad through the Sahara Desert, and then to Syria, then a small trip to Beirut. It sounded extremely scary and dangerous, and all the girls very warily stepped onto the old bedraggled bus with our hearts in our mouths. How we got through is unbelievable; a hot bus, sand everywhere and a tired Egyptian bus driver... most of it I have conveniently forgotten...

CHAPTER EIGHT

My wedding day...

Little had I ever dreamed of a wedding day in Beirut ... being married by a bearded turban-headed Moslem Sheikh!

The day dawned bright, with a cloudless sky. I dressed slowly in a white silk brocade dress with a white lacy shawl covering my hair and waited anxiously for my handsome man to return with the Sheikh. Suddenly, a young attractive Lebanese girl came to the door, whom I had never seen before. Kadiche and Emmina barred her way, and spoke rapidly in Arabic. She looked shocked and ran down the stairs, looking distraught.

"Who was that?" I enquired.

Both sisters brushed my questions aside quickly, and began babbling at breakneck speed in Arabic. They explained to me that it was their aunt and that she was surprised about the impending nuptials. Somehow, I didn't believe them, but I could sense this was the only explanation I would get, and was soon distracted with our special day.

Strong black coffee and sweet cakes were passed around, and at last, footsteps could be heard on the stairs, and in walked a white bearded old man dressed in the religious clothes of a Sheikh.

And then it began – the ceremony, all in Arabic, some English translated by Tarek, was performed, and we were married.

Tarek ran into the kitchen and returned carrying an ice-cold bottle of champagne. I was amazed, as I knew nobody in the family drank because of their religion, and frowned upon it. He had brought it especially for me on our day. He warmly kissed me again, and we clicked our glasses together, and repeated the words of love in Arabic and English.

Everyone congratulated us, and the Sheikh slowly and meticulously started writing out the marriage document in Arabic, he shook our hands, muttering and complaining why he had been forced to do this ceremony, especially to an Infidel. We both signed it, and he eventually left, still muttering...

I knew the Father and Mother were still in the mountains, and I was very curious as to their reaction when they heard of their son's marriage, when he told them. I realized our honeymoon would be spent in Beirut, enjoying the sandy beaches, scenic countryside, and restaurants. It is full of hideaways, international restaurants, and romantic spots ideal for tourists or newlyweds. Relaxed days were spent walking and talking on the beach, and our nights were hours of earth-shattering love making. His good looks, and bronzed body-building physique caused a mild stirring amongst all the girls, and they all turned to take a second glance. I loved it, and felt proud.

I adored the people and their fantastic hospitality, generosity and warm nature. There were two sides to Beirut.

The real old Arab downtown part, full of intriguing bazaars, hoards of people elbow to elbow, hooting horns and the usual chaotic traffic. Gold markets, shoe markets, clothes markets, each individual type of store were clustered together, not spread around, but one right next to the other. Strolling through the many winding alleyways of the gold market, on both sides of you, glass windows overflowed with gold bracelets, rings, necklaces, and every type of jewellery you could ever want. The souks had fish and hanging meat and chicken carcases, full of flies (not appetizing) and barrow upon barrow of fresh vegetables and fruits were bartered to eager, haggling buyers. All produce was grown in the mountain villages and sold in the streets.

CHAPTER NINE

The other Beirut, the Cosmopolitan side, was full of high-rises, and was modern and new with French-like sidewalk cafes, lavishly decorated ornate cinemas and small expensive boutiques stocking clothes from many countries. For the gourmet, international cuisines in authentic restaurants flourished, as well as world-wide entertainment. Walking along Hamra Street, every accent, dialect and language could be heard from all around the world. The beaches were full of girls in string bikinis but a few miles away, many of the girls were not permitted to remove their headscarf outside the house.

One evening, after a sun-drenched day on "The Riviera" beach, we returned home, and Tarek suggested we visit "The Casino Du Liban" that evening, and promised it was one of the best shows in the world. Dressing excitedly in a long black shimmering dress, clutch bag and shoes to match, I waited anxiously for Tarek. He walked into the sitting room, looking magnificent in a silver grey smoking jacket and contrasting slacks. He put his arm around me.

"This show is supposed to be better than Las Vegas", he said jokingly. "You will be amazed at the gambling machines, the show and the size of the auditorium."

"I'm really looking forward to it", I replied. "It will be nice to see another show, and not be performing in it." He scowled slightly, not wanting to be reminded of my past.

We hailed a passing cab, and after about an hour's journey along a beautiful palm-laden shoreline, I saw ahead of me a magnificent sight - a very large two turreted castle-like structure, massive in size. Large landscaped courtyards stretched out onto long balconies which looked out over the jagged rocks and blue Mediterranean Sea. This was "The Casino Du Liban".

A valet ran out to open our door, and we walked inside. The noise and clatter of gambling slot machines filled our ears, and pleasant sounding music wafted its way around the room. We were escorted to our table in an enormous showroom, and took our seats. The stage was massive and wove its way in passages through the audience, and it seemed to me large enough for an elephant! How right I was.

With a resounding overture, the velvet blue curtains opened. It was electrifying, and as the finale began to unfold, an elephant did walk slowly onto the stage, as showgirls descended from the ceiling on whirling poles in record numbers. Tarek and I held hands, and as I gazed around the entire room, I couldn't see any other man more handsome or desirable. My gaze stopped, and I looked again and then froze. About two tables away, with only eyes for each other, Omar and Lila sat, oblivious to the world. "What on earth are they doing here?" I thought.

All the artists received a standing ovation, and we stood up to leave, to wander to the many other gambling rooms. Moving Tarek as far away from Omar and Lila as I could, we walked towards the lift. Each gambling floor was regulated by wealth and stakes, and a special identification card was required to enter. Many Sheikhs, with flowing white robes from Saudi Arabia, Kuwait Dubai, and the United Arab Emirates, were bent over the tables in serious demanding concentration.

I was tapped abruptly on the shoulder, and as I spun around, there stood a grinning Omar, and a smiling Lila, looking enquiringly at my handsome escort. I threw my arms around them, and hugged them both.

"It's wonderful to see you both, but what are you doing in Beirut?"

"We are here to see the show, as obviously, so are you", he said, with eyebrows raised waiting for an introduction.

Pulling Tarek towards me, "Omar and Lila, this is my husband, Tarek Eddine." Their mouths dropped open, and Tarek gave them a curious and puzzled look. Tarek shook hands with them, and they chatted gaily on about Cairo, and "Sahara City". Unobtrusively, I gave Lila my telephone number, and told her to call me, and we could chat more. Laughing gaily, they walked away arm in arm.

"Where did you meet those two?" Tarek asked inquisitively. A battery of questions came one after another and I tried to calm him down.

"Are those two married?" he asked.

"No, they are just friends, and old sweethearts."

"Anyway, in future, please don't go around hugging anyone, especially men. It's not done here unless it's a close relative. People will misunderstand your intentions. You must learn to be more careful." I looked at his grave face, and wondered how long my adjustment would take.

The remainder of the evening was spent dancing cheek-to-cheek with my husband, and after a moonlight drive, we arrived at his parents' house, tired and exhausted after a romantic-filled evening.

CHAPTER TEN

The day arrived for Tarek to register the marriage, because without this, the ceremony by the Sheikh is invalid in the Moslem religion.

Downtown was not one of my favourite places, but that's where all the religious and civil offices were located. I hated the grim old buildings with their dismal, cluttered appearance. Waiting nervously in the lobby, there was a loud noise from within. Tarek crashed open the door screaming in Arabic to the official inside. Not saying a word, I waited for him to calm down. Arriving back at his home, he told me angrily the Managers of the show had filed a complaint against me for leaving and breaking the entertainment contract, and was trying to make it as difficult as possible to register the marriage. I burst into tears, and Tarek wrapped his large arms around me.

"Don't worry, darling. I will take care of it tomorrow, I promise you." I felt again the warm protected and trusting feeling of our very first meeting. I knew he would.

I spent a sleepless night tossing and turning, wondering what would happen the following day. Tarek left bright and early in the morning, and was soon back with a smile of achievement on his face. As I thought, he was able to overcome all the difficulties, and the Managers eventually withdrew the complaint. We were now officially husband and wife....

Day by day, living under the same roof with his family was becoming impossible. I still could not understand a word they said, and vice versa, unless Tarek was there to translate.

I soon found out no more bikinis or short dresses. What was accepted during courting and before marriage, was not accepted after. I had already experienced a lot of Tarek's jealousy, and realized he put no trust in women at all. Natural gestures and movements I would make with friends were chastised and curbed.

Each morning dressed exquisitely in one of his many tailor-made suits, he would go on interviews, looking for a job as a pilot. I was hoping this was not going to take too long, as I dearly craved a home of my own, and privacy away from the parents, brothers, sisters, and countless relatives.

That evening, after leaving a downtown cinema, we were strolling in the Bourge glancing at the various shops on either side. A young man walked by, and glanced at me in passing. Without any warning, Tarek picked him up, and threw him bodily through the nearby glass window of a shop on the corner of the street! I just stood there, speechless.

"Why did you do that?!" I shouted.

"I didn't like the way he looked at you", he replied casually.

In a couple of seconds, a taxi screamed to a halt and at the wheel was one of the many relatives. He screamed something to Tarek, and I was hurled headlong into the back of the taxi. We took off at break-neck speed, as police sirens could be heard approaching.

Nothing was discussed about this, and I realized Tarek thought this was quite the normal thing to do.

A couple of days later, we decided it was time to return to our first meeting place, Long Beach. The taxi drove up to the beach and we both stepped out and immediately a shouting match between the cab driver and Tarek began. In a flash, Tarek ran to the front of the cab and dragged the taxi driver out by the scruff of his neck. A fight started, and Tarek knocked him to the ground. I again just stood there, not comprehending what was going on!! He straightened his tie, dusted off his blazer, adjusted his crease-lined white pants, and took my arm, nonchalantly sauntering through the entrance. I looked at him in amazement.

"What happened this time?"

"Well, he tried to charge me double fare, thinking I was with a European tourist, and wanted to impress her, and normally he would get away with it, but I don't like our people being cheaters."

I knew the cab driver would be more careful with his future fares. We separated to our different changing facilities, and met again on the beach. Sitting side by side in the blazing sun in our chaises, looking out again at the rocks, I looked up into his virile face.

"Why don't we hire a small rowing boat today, Tarek and find one of those secluded coves and beaches?" He looked at me, embarrassed.

"What are you thinking about Julie? What if others have the same idea?"

"Let's try anyway."

We ran over to the docking area, and hired a small rowing boat, throwing suntan lotion and towels under the seat, as we pushed it out into the deep water. We rowed around in the blazing sun, until I saw a little cove and cave I spotted many times before. Both jumping out, Tarek beached the boat, and we ran up onto the beach. Spreading our towels on the white sand, there was not a soul in sight, and we had the whole tiny beach and cove to ourselves. I leaned over closely to Tarek.

"Would you like me to smother you with lotion?"

"You know I never burn, Julie, but let me get your back, it looks a little red."

As he gently massaged my back, I suddenly turned and we exchanged a passionate kiss. His massaging continued, and without hesitation, we both pulled off our suits, and stood there in our naked glory. He gently touched my cheek and hair, and with wild abandon, again consummated our love.

CHAPTER ELEVEN

Later that evening, glowing with health from sun and love, we were lounging on the balcony, munching contentedly on a wide variety of wonderful fruits grown locally. The one thing I needed no adjustment to was the food. It was delicious, healthy and satisfying. Nothing was ever eaten from a can, it was always fresh and took hours to prepare. I was worried how I was going to be able to manage to cook this food once we did have an apartment of our own. Fruit and vegetables were so cheap and plentiful, but the fun and challenge to me was in the bargaining. I hoped one day I could speak enough Arabic to be able to bargain for everything, as the locals did.

As we were relaxing, Tarek turned and took my hand.

"Another thing, Julie. Please don't talk to any men on the streets, even if they are friends of mine, and never, never invite them in if I am not here."

"But why not?" I asked naively.

"Unfortunately, they will exaggerate the conversation and enlarge on everything that took place, and then it will become a scandal. I know this is a lot for you to understand, but it will make your life easier here if you can remember all of these rules."

The next day, hand in hand, returning home after spending a fascinating afternoon at the souks, the same Lebanese girl from our wedding day was waiting to see Tarek. I looked at him suspiciously.

"That's not your aunt, is it? She is much too young." I knew this explanation didn't make sense when I was told who she was on our wedding day.

"No, you're right. She was my girlfriend for two years."

He continued telling me they were sweethearts, but after not seeing him for three weeks, she thought he had left town. Stopping by the house to check, she had been barred from entering by his two sisters, only to be told her boyfriend was getting married. Tarek said a few words to her, and she came over and congratulated me, and walked away sadly ... I wondered how many other girls had been so disillusioned.

The days, weeks and months melted into one frenzied passion. Three months after our marriage, I found myself pregnant. Tarek was ecstatic when I told him the news, and picked me up and swung me around in a surge of wild emotion. I loved children too, but needed a separate identity away from the clan, just him and our new baby.

At last, a few weeks later, walking into the bedroom with a smug smile, I knew he had somehow landed a pilot's position.

"Well, I have a First Officer's position with TMA, and I am going to start immediately. Isn't that wonderful?" His English had improved so dramatically in the last six months that there was only a slight intriguing accent left. Hugging and kissing, I congratulated him, and heaved a sigh of relief.

Before we could even begin apartment hunting, my dreams were cruelly shattered, as returning from the airline office for lunch a few days later, he sadly told me he was being transferred to India for around six months. His orders were to transport cargo between India and Pakistan. I looked at him bewildered.

"What shall I do now? I can't possibly stay here with your parents, Tarek. I would go crazy, and we cannot even converse." Hugging me closely to his chest, he looked worried.

"I know, Julie, but where else would you go? I want someone taking care of you while I am away."

Thinking it over for a few minutes even though I hated the idea, my Step-Grandmother was still in Bristol, and I could stay with her until my child was born. At least we spoke the same language. Sitting down, I wrote a short letter to her asking her if this arrangement was convenient.

"I hate to think of you having the baby on your own. I should be there with you, but it looks impossible." His voice broke with emotion, and I clasped his muscular body closer.

"There is really nothing you can do about it darling. I am used to taking care of myself, and I can be regularly checked by the doctor there and have the best care."

I knew I would have to be brave and frugal, as we needed to save as much as possible to set up house when I returned.

The dreaded day of departure arrived. Driving to the airport, hands tightly entwined, I gazed through moistened eyes for the last time for a while at the city I had grown to love. Tarek dressed in his pilot's uniform and hat, and looked just good enough to eat, and my heart was heavy. We both stepped out of the taxi at Beirut International, and I walked wearily into the airport. Flying on the company's plane, a DC8, was not going to be fun. Clutching my Arab love for the last time, and feeling his heart beating against my chest, I walked slowly to the waiting plane.

The flight was worse than I thought. Three months pregnant and the bumpy ride left me spending many of the hours in the bathroom being sick. After an exhausting 14 hours, and feeling terrible, the plane arrived in Frankfurt. Transferring to a passenger airline was sheer heaven and an hour later, I landed in London ...

CHAPTER TWELVE

A rainy cold day and dull misty skies greeted me as I walked down the ramp at Heathrow Airport. A slow drizzle was falling, the first rain I had seen in months. The old familiar undergrounds, smells sights and sounds brought me back to the reality of my country, customs and heritage. Losing my way on the underground, I soon found Paddington Station, and stepped on the train for the too familiar ride to my old hometown. The journey and taxi ride to my Grandmother's familiar house completely exhausted me, and I wearily walked up the path to the home I had been so glad to leave.

Waiting for the baby – and waiting for Tarek's letters – seemed to go on forever. My pregnancy began to show, and I missed already the comfort, companionship, love and understanding of my husband. Visiting the doctor, he checked my progress, and prescribed all sorts of vitamins, milk and exercise.

Doreen, a tiny vivacious redhead whom I had known as a teenager, became a comforter and confidant during this difficult period. We spent pleasant evenings on the town, shopping, seeing a movie and walking together on the Clifton Downs. She was also fascinated to hear about Tarek, as was my Grandmother, who kept asking every day when he would be visiting!

"I can't wait to see this fabulous volatile man" Doreen said.

"When he does come, let's all go out together for dinner and drinks."

I numbly nodded, hoping it would be soon.

Opening up his letter the next morning, my hand shook, as Tarek wrote of another TMA's plane crash. He casually mentioned it at the bottom of his letter saying he just returned from visiting the bereaved family's home.

"Oh God, please take care of him, he thinks he is so indestructible." I said out loud.

Another letter came a few days later, saying he could at last get away for a few days to visit, and would telephone on his arrival in London.

Dreaming about my "fantasy marriage" in Beirut, and my complete lack of understanding of the meaning of the words of the ceremony, I was determined to persuade my love to marry me again in my own hometown for my own peace of mind. Even though I was six months pregnant, I wanted to hear those poignant words in English, and be able to understand and respond, and feel the special moment. I hoped it could be arranged.

The sun peeked through the sky for a second, and accidentally peering through the bay windows, I saw a taxi come to a sudden halt. Out stepped my Arab warrior, striding up the path, forceful and aggressive. I ran out, screaming out to my Grandmother he had arrived. He embraced me, and then swept my Grandmother up in his arms – he had already taken her heart. She couldn't wait to invite all the relatives and friends to meet him, show him off, and have a celebration. We managed a special evening with Doreen and her boyfriend, and later that evening, entered my teenage bedroom. I remembered well so many nights spent alone in this room, but I knew this would be very special, sharing this with the man I adored, and whose child I was carrying.

He seemed a little hesitant and shy, as he had been on our first meeting, and my massive bulk presented a very different picture from our first night of love. He gazed at me longingly.

"It has been too long darling; it has been hard for me. You seem to glow with motherhood." Personally, I thought I looked like a big bloated cow, but didn't want to shatter the moment.

He felt my stomach and then jumped back, as if he had received an electric shock.

"I felt him move" he said.

"Him?" I questioned. "The baby is always active, especially at night."

"I know it's a boy."

I laughed. Typical, I thought. I noticed in Beirut when a son was born, great jubilation took place and cigars were handed around indiscriminately. But on the other hand, when a girl was born, nothing was said unless you specifically asked. I touched his cheek gently, and caressed his back and neck.

"I really would feel better and more secure, Tarek, if we got married here in Bristol", I said tentatively.

"Why, you don't think it was legal in Beirut?" he said frowning.

"Oh, that's not the point. I just couldn't understand everything, that was the problem."

He smiled. "Yes it must have been a most unusual wedding for you. Of course if it makes you feel better, I will."

We kissed passionately, and he gently caressed the outline of my body, and we fell on the bed.

"I am so afraid I will hurt the baby if we make love", he said shyly.

"No, I checked with the doctor, and it is perfectly safe."

He groaned and all my pent up feelings of want and desire flamed, and then we were quenched by his unquestionable manliness.

CHAPTER THIRTEEN

Again, my wedding day. (At least this time not by a Sheikh, and in a language I understood), but this time under English cloudy skies. I prayed the sun would show through for just a few moments. I dressed in my most flattering maternity outfit and comfortable shoes. Tarek dressed in his pilot's uniform and hat and looked gorgeous, and just before leaving, my Grandmother securely pinned a carnation in his buttonhole. My two aunts accompanied us to the Bristol Registry Office, and we waited anxiously for our turn. I watched with amusement the startled gazes of some of the clerks and officials, as they quickly averted their eyes from my expansive stomach and sniggered.

I nudged Tarek. "I bet they think this is a shot-gun wedding."

"What is a shot-gun wedding?" Tarek asked enquiringly, eyebrows raised.

"Well, it means we had to get married because you made me pregnant and you are forced to be here, usually with my relatives aiming a shot-gun at you. That's how it used to be in the olden days, so I am told."

He stood up angrily, looking furious....

"I am going to make sure this Registrar knows about our wedding in Beirut, and he will write it down on our marriage certificate. I don't want my son thinking he is illegitimate, that will not happen.

At last, the official beckoned us. We stood quietly, and together we again heard the words of love and commitment, this time understandable. I looked lovingly at him, and could not imagine life without him in it. He answered warmly and clearly, and then the Registrar said:

"I now pronounce you man and wife."

"You may kiss the Bride."...he tenderly kissed my lips, and hand in hand, we walked out of the office. The Registrar and Aunts congratulating us.

Tarek shut the door purposely, and arms gesturing madly in the air, he strode back into the office, to tell the official he wanted the information of our previous wedding in July 1961 to be written clearly on the marriage certificate. He continued talking rapidly, explaining to the Registrar our previous ceremony in Beirut was entirely in Arabic. and I obviously had not understood the words spoken, and he was doing this for me. The Registrar nodded, not really quite comprehending the story, but looking at Tarek's anxious and angry face, and not wishing to be harassed any further, hurriedly wrote down all the information and we both signed the document.

The following day, Tarek was scheduled to leave, and my heart ached for him to remain with me until the baby was born.

"I have found out Julie, you can come back six weeks after the boy, (he was still convinced it was a boy, so I said nothing,) is born, so by that time I will have an apartment ready, and everything prepared for you."

Returning to Apsley Road, we had a small celebration and as the evening came to an end, I knew this would be the last time for a while, I would feel the warmth of his body against mine.

We retired early, and Tarek, still shy, snuggled close.

"I cannot wait to return to Beirut, darling. You don't know how much I miss it."

"You do? How do you think I feel Julie? I only have a couple of months left of this flying between India and Pakistan, and then I can go back home again."

He touched my stomach again.

"I know you are going to have a boy. What will we call him?"

"Well, let's wait and see", I replied teasingly, running my fingers across his tanned muscular chest.

"I think we can compromise on names. You should also think about some attractive girls names."

"No, I won't, I have no doubt about it", he replied. I shook my head – nothing daunted his belief.

Our last night together was spent in close intimacy, and as the dawn welcomed a new day, it was time again to travel back with him to Temple Meads Station. The last thing I saw through my torrent of tears was the train steaming out of the station, and the white handkerchief waving dismally in the air. My love was gone again.

CHAPTER FOURTEEN

The months of confinement came to an end, and at last the estimated date of my child's arrival was here ... but nothing. Ten days went slowly and aimlessly by, and calling on the phone, I begged and pleaded with the hospital staff to please force the birth, as the baby was not in any hurry to get here on his own.

The twelve hours of pain was the longest hours I have ever spent, but at long last on July 6th, 1962 my 9 pound baby boy lay in my arms. No gas, air, or injections for me, not allowed under National Health, unless you were having a breach, but I was having a normal natural birth. After delivery, looking at him nestled in my arms, and sipping the best cup of tea I have ever tasted in my life, I wished my husband could have been a witness to this miracle of life.

My first early visitors were my Grandmother, Aunts and Uncles, who couldn't wait to catch a glimpse of the baby in the nursery. I still had no idea what to call him, but knew I didn't have much time, as the birth certificate needed to be completed. Lying in the hospital bed, I opened up one of Tarek's latest letters, and noticed he wrote that he thought it was fair if I named the first, and he would name the second –

one European name, and one Lebanese. As I was in England, I should name the first.

My Grandmother hurriedly sent off a telegram to Tarek telling him the good news. She wrote:

9 lb boy born July 6th, Mother and Son well.

I wish I could have seen his face and smiled at his "I told you so" expression. Lying in the next bed, I became friends with another young girl who was recently a new mother as well. In idle conversation, she mentioned her other child's name was Darren. I liked the name, and thought Tarek would approve, so quickly writing to him, told him about the name I was thinking about calling the baby.

After ten miserable boring long days, putting up with cold and harsh Nurses shouting...

"You definitely can pee" (even though I had endured a lot of painful stitches, due to his size), I was at last given permission to leave the hospital. Nervously holding my new son, wrapped in his new white shawl, personal advice on husbands and motherhood ringing in my ears from a concerned and stern matron, I took a taxi home.

There was so much to do before I left – prepare my passport, birth certificate, and apply for the tickets. Also a very important goal was to get fitted for a coil to prevent pregnancy again, knowing that Moslems do not believe in birth control. "God (Allah) will provide" was the saying I heard as more and more children were born.

I took care of this without a problem, and obtained the cream and lovingly and with great care, packed it into my suitcase (I was not going to get pregnant again quickly????? No birth control pills or condoms there...

Doreen and I spent many happy hours together with the baby, and she babysat many times with my screaming son to get me out of the house. No washer or dryer, meant washing the crap out of the nappies, in the toilet (that is diapers), then washing them and hanging them out to drive on a line in the garden, even though it was cold and usually raining.....in July, mind you, was a nightmare, plus no sleep at night. because Darren woke up many times in the night and was wearing me out. Also boiling everything, as I was told to give him some formula as well as breast milk, was exhausting. Six weeks to the day, after completing everything, and receiving the plane tickets through the mail, I gathered my suitcases together, wrapped up my precious son in the same white shawl, and stepped into the taxi for my trip to the familiar old Temple Meads station, where I had said my last farewell to my love.

Knowing how unreliable and slow the mail was in Lebanon, I had written to Tarek three weeks earlier, (no phones there) telling him of my arrival date and time. The flight was long, but Darren slept soundly all the way. At last, peering through the aisle window, I saw with impending excitement and thrill the outline of the scenic beaches and high-rises, and as we descended, my heart began racing at the thought of seeing my man again, and all three of us being together ... home at last.

CHAPTER FIFTEEN

Stepping down the the ramp carefully, I looked around anxiously for my Arab warrior, but no sign. Very upset, I saw some TMA employees standing around. Running up to them, I asked for their help, and they hurriedly bundled us into one of TMA's vans, and off we sped at the usual suicide speed to Tarek's mother and father's house.

Climbing those unpleasant steps, I knocked loudly on the door. Achmid, his younger brother, opened the door, looking startled to see me. Kadiche and Zanab ran from the kitchen to embrace me, babbling in Arabic. Trying as hard as I could in the little Arabic I now knew, I tried to make them understand to go and find Tarek. Amid more shouting and pointing, Achmid ran out of the door. Oohing and aahing over Darren, the two sisters were oblivious to my increasing anger.

Eventually, after my anger had reached a crescendo the door was pushed open and in strode Tarek, looking frantic. He hugged me, embarrassed by the staring onlookers, and then bent down and looked at his son for the first time.

"Why weren't you at the airport?" I shouted, really mad.

"I didn't know you were coming! Why didn't you let me know?" he screamed back.

"Three weeks ago, I sent you a letter to let you know when I was coming. Do you mean to say you never received it?" (What a surprise)?

By this time, the whole family were gathered around, eyes wide, watching the confrontation. I calmed down, and we looked at each other intensely, and my anger and frustrations slowly died down. He looked down again at Darren, and gathered him up in his arms.

"Well, Julie, this one is for you – blond hair and blue eyes"

"Hair and eye colour do change you know, sometimes within six weeks, I laughingly answered

He picked up his son lovingly, said farewell to his family, and we took off for our new apartment.

He again reassured me he had completely furnished and decorated it, and teasingly hoped I would like his choices and appreciate his taste.

I hoped and prayed that now nothing would stop our having a beautiful and contented life together...

Our first evening alone was sheer heaven. Tarek ran to the local grocery store and bought a bottle of my favourite white wine, and found some cheese, olives, and local Arabic bread. Looking around, I was impressed how well he had furnished the apartment, and noticed in the kitchen all the crockery and utensils I needed. There were two bedrooms, living room, and dining room, and walking on the long balcony outside, I saw it overlooked the Hamra area of Beirut.

He came out of the bedroom in his red silk bathrobe, and handed me a goblet of cold wine. We both leaned against the balcony and looked over. He turned to me tenderly

"I cannot believe you are back with our baby son." His sheer animal presence and masculinity filled the night air. Hand in hand, we sauntered back into our sitting room. I watching him sitting so comfortably in his sexy red silk robe, his tanned leg hooked over the side, and going to the bedroom, I slipped into a new midnight blue chiffon negligee.

"I do love what you have bought, and you do have good taste. The colours and styles are great."

"Actually, it was fun. I didn't think it would be." His eyes crinkled, and he pulled me towards him onto the couch. There was no expansive stomach to intrude, and the feel of his muscular body heightened my desire and swept me away in a heat of passion. His love-making was as it had been on the first days of our "kismet" encounter, frenzied and without end, and lying in his arms in my new home, amid new surroundings, seemed like paradise.

From the night we moved in, there was a constant ringing of the doorbell. All the relatives from great aunties to distant cousins descended on us like vultures on their prey, to congratulate us on our newborn son. Coffee and cakes had to be available, and the endless hours of constant Arabic was beginning to drive me crazy. If I could have joined in the conversation, it would not have been so bad, but they spoke so quickly in Arabic that it was impossible for Tarek to translate everything.

I longed to go out for dinner with my husband alone, just the two of us – was that too much to ask?

That very next evening, we had an evening planned, and Zanab was already taking care of Darren. Made up and ready to leave in a pink gown – one of Tarek's favourites – he stood by the front door in an Italian cut blue serge suit ready to leave, when the piercing sound of the doorbell interrupted the silence.

"I cannot stand another evening of Arabic!" I screamed. "Please tell them to go away, telephone first, and see if it is convenient to come over. I'll go crazy if this goes on."

I looked at Zanab standing nearby, looking frightened to death at my loud and angry tone.

I rushed into the bedroom and slammed the door. From within, I could hear Arabic salutations being exchanged with some relative I had never seen before. I just flung myself on the bed in sheer frustration. The bedroom door was flung open, and Tarek stood there, looking very mad.

"You have to come out and greet them, otherwise they will consider you very rude, and this will shame me." He bent forward dragging my arm forcibly.

"How about shaming me? Why can't they call beforehand, like anyone else?" I shouted back.

Shaking with rage, Tarek said "It is not the custom here to do that. I have tried to explain to you our different ways. Even if I explain you are from another culture, with certain rules, they will not understand them, as you are living here, not in England. So get up and come out, right now!" He dragged me off the bed, and with a fixed smile on my face, I walked reluctantly into the sitting room.

The endless evening finally came to a close, with Tarek trying valiantly to translate every word of the conversations.

CHAPTER SIXTEEN

The following day, Tarek's mother was coming over to try and teach me the Arabic food that I would have to learn to cook.

Shariffa (one of her daughter's names) was a good-looking, tall, well-built woman, very strong and quite forbidding, and wore the traditional covering over her head. As she had been to the Hajj, the Moslem holy area in Saudi Arabia, she was entitled to wear this white headgear, and to be addressed as Hajj Shariffa. Anyone visiting the holy sanctuary was entitled to this form of religious respect.

Out of all her children, 10 who had lived, and two which died, I knew instinctively that Tarek was her favourite. The way she talked to him, touched him, and spoke, were very strong indications of her feelings. I knew she must have been dismayed at the news of his marriage to a foreign infidel woman from England, but had resigned herself to having to accept exactly what her favourite son wanted – she knew with him, there was no choice.

Arriving bright and early, with bags and bags of groceries, she took over and began checking closets, and opening drawers. Tarek had left already for his airline office, so nodding and shaking my head at what

I thought might be an appropriate time, she proceeded to cook. Gesturing, pointing, and showing, she tried hard to make me understand how to cook, Lebanese style. As far as I could see, it seemed to take all morning to make one dish, and combined with the baby and housework, I could see where the saying "barefoot and pregnant" originated!

As soon as Tarek returned for lunch, I asked him to please thank her for her time and trouble. She beamed, and leaving behind enough dishes for a week, took off.

I found it hard to understand that some Arabic men still believe cooking, washing-up, or any kind of household chores unmanly, and only women's work. Tarek would never attempt to help in the kitchen, go into the kitchen, or do any kind of housework; this was not part of their culture and completely demeaning.

One Saturday afternoon, I was visiting some of my friends, pilot's wives, mostly Europeans, and was enjoying a good conversation, and delicious English tea. Tarek arrived promptly at the door to pick me up. Darren was in his baby carriage, and it was such a warm clear day, we decided to walk along the Corniche Mezzra on the beachfront.

Strolling along pushing the carriage, I turned to him quietly and asked him to please push it for a second, as I wanted to cool my feet in the nearby ocean. I could not believe my ears when he turned to me quite bluntly and said

"No, I won't."

I thought for a moment my hearing was impaired!

"What? This is considered normal behaviour in Europe, Tarek. I have seen hundreds of fathers out walking their children, some pushing large prams and carriages. Why can't you?"

By this time, we were both screaming and passing onlookers were staring at us in surprise.

"I know this, Julie", he screamed "but here if they saw me do this, I would not be considered a man. If I was in Europe, it would be different, but we are not."

We were both very angry by now, and his look was thunderous as he strode off, leaving Darren and I to walk home alone. Strolling on, forcing the tears back, I was upset and furious. I wondered if I would ever understand his attitude towards these kinds of things.

His flying schedule increased, and I began to feel very lonesome. One evening, sitting alone watching another old re-run of "I Love Lucy" on the TV I only had three channels, mostly in Arabic the doorbell rang. I opened it to find an old flying friend of Tarek's, Samir, standing there.

"Is Tarek here?" he asked. Knowing him very well from many other social occasions, I invited him in for coffee

"No, he's away flying this evening Samir, but do come in and sit for a while."

We spent a delightful hour enjoying each other's company, and then it was time for him to leave. He thanked me for the coffee, and as he left, told me to tell Tarek he had stopped by and to give him a call. I promised I would.

The next day, I prepared one of Tarek's favourite Lebanese dishes (Wora Anab) – grape leaves stuffed with rice and meat, and was feeling quite proud of my accomplishment.

Suddenly, the door was flung open, and Tarek stormed into the house, looking as though he was going to annihilate me.

"What is this I hear about a man being in the house while I was away?"

I had to think for a minute who it was. I just couldn't remember.

"What man?" I asked stupidly.

"I just saw Samir at the office, and he told me he passed by last night, and stayed with you for over an hour."

"So?" I asked.

His face began to get red and he started screaming and gesturing.

"I told you never, never, to invite any man into the house if I am not here", he screamed, throwing his arms up in desperation.

"The people upstairs and downstairs will talk, and you will be considered a loose woman, and not to be trusted."

In his rage, he pushed me savagely, and as tears started to fall, he stormed out, and the house shook as he slammed the door.

CHAPTER SEVENTEEN

The months passed, and my adjustment continued. I laughed hysterically at the film I once saw called "The Americanization of Emily", and thought they wouldn't believe "The Middle Easternization of Julie"!

Darren was five months old when I realized I was pregnant again. Trying to insert the coil and the ointment at romantic moments proved to be such a chore, but of course, I had obviously not done it all the time, so here I was pregnant again, I didn't feel I could handle another pregnancy and baby so soon, and pleading with Tarek, asked him if something could be done. Rather surprised at his attitude, he promised he would take me to a doctor very soon to have a series of injections. He kept his word, but nothing happened. My stomach was still expanding.

One evening over dinner, I asked him point blank.

"What were those injections Dr. Habbash gave me, Tarek?"

He looked at me with a smirk on his face.

"Did you really think I would let you destroy my child? Those were vitamin injections, Julie. I would never kill an unborn baby, you should know that."

He got up from the table and walked into the sitting room to lounge in his favourite chair, looking amazingly handsome in his red silk robe.

"Do you think it is wise to have another baby so soon, Tarek? Darren is still a baby." He caught my hand, and pulled me towards him.

"We can manage, Julie. This is God's will he will provide" I sighed inwardly, I decided not to tackle that one, I had heard it too many times before. I sadly walked back into the kitchen to wash up.

The following Saturday, his company had invited all their employees for a cocktail party. It was to take place in one of the luxury hotels, "La Vendome", and I was looking forward to meeting Tarek's co-workers, and the captains he flew with so often, and their wives. I was thrilled to be able to dress up, do some dancing, and have some fun.

Tarek strolled in at lunch time and we sat down for Kibbe, a local Lebanese dish. We were nearly finished eating, then I casually mentioned I was going to the hairdressers at 2 p.m. He suddenly jumped up, looking fierce.

"Is the hairdresser male or female?" he demanded

"I don't know which one will do it, Tarek. Why?" I asked, not having any idea.

"I don't want any man touching your hair. Do you understand?"

Smiling warmly "You've got to be joking, right?" Looking at his red face, I knew this was no joke.

"Well don't worry, I will make sure the lady does it, alright??"

Appeased, he sat down again, and continued eating.

Later that evening, even though I was three months pregnant, I managed to fit into a midnight blue cocktail dress. Tarek emerged from the bedroom in his silver-grey tuxedo and contrasting slacks, and looked gorgeous, but his expression was not happy.

"I suppose we have to go to this thing, but you know I hate parties."

"Well, I'm looking forward to it", I replied.

He scrutinized my appearance and complimented me on my dress and hair, and took me in his arms.

"I know I am difficult, but it is as hard for me to adjust to your ways as it is for you to adjust to mine. We just need love and time."

We drove off in Tarek's car and arriving at the imposing hotel, the door was opened by the waiting valet. The party was in full swing, and we both soon began chatting with his co-workers and friends.

Mountains of delicious Lebanese food were arranged around the suite, and soft ballroom music filled the air. Standing at the bar conversing with one of the Captain's wives, Joanne, a rose suddenly landed on the bar in front of me. I glanced up and caught the eye of one of the Directors, who smiled and winked and raised his glass in a complimentary toast. Dining and dancing the evening away, and socializing with the many employees of TMA was fun. A few short personal speeches from the Directors, and then Tarek and I said our goodbyes. As we walked towards the elevator, I tried to put my arm through Tarek's, and was hurt and shocked when he pushed me away, looking sullen and extremely angry.

We descended in the elevator in complete silence. As we waited for our car to be delivered, I turned to him and said

"What is the matter, Tarek?"

"You should know what is the matter. You were flirting with Bob Townsend and he threw you a rose."

'Oh, you arrogant, jealous Arab', I thought to myself

"I was not interested in him at all", I retorted. "You have to be sociable at a cocktail party."

Driving home in complete silence, I could see it was pointless to try to explain further. I hoped after a night's sleep, he would recover from my terrible misdeed.

There is no question or debate in the Arabic household who is the boss. Forget any women's lib, or equal rights. He is the boss and that is that. Don't even try to change it, you have everything to lose, including your children, as all Moslem laws favour them way down the line. Their belief, even as late as the early 1960's, women are weak creatures who should be protected, are not intelligent, and certainly cannot be trusted. These prejudices, plus his upbringing, are something that would take many years to change, if it ever did.

Without air-conditioning in the apartment, the heat of the summer became oppressive, and I longed for September to arrive to deliver. The temperature, actually was only between 75 and 85, but with my added weight and bulk, the stairs leading up to our apartment seemed to take longer and longer.

His parents, as was customary, retreated to the mountains, and the city was quiet and mellow. Having now found a few other English and European girlfriends, I spent many pleasant afternoons sipping tea and chatting about our various lives, and our adjustments.

Tarek was flying more and more, and was challenged and thrilled to be doing something he dearly and obviously loved.

It was a clear cool early Sunday morning on September 15th in 1963 that I started to have labour pains. Feeling thankful that Tarek was here, this time and not in some other foreign country, and not flying, he carried my suitcase down to the car and speeded recklessly and frantically towards the French Hospital.

Making sure I was safely installed in a private room, (totally different from the UK National Health) he left immediately, expecting it to be many hours before the new arrival would emerge.

Given all the help I asked for – gas, plus injections – not deemed necessary in England, a few short hours later, I heard a lusty cry. Looking down in awe, I saw this long black-haired red-faced thing emerging, and lo and behold, another penis! The red-faced black-haired boy weighed in at 10 lbs, and he certainly looked the living image of my Lebanese love.

A few hours later, Tarek dashed into the hospital, carrying a bunch of flowers, kissed me lightly, and looked down at his image. His eyes grew misty, and gazing again, he whispered quietly,

"I don't mind dying now. I have someone just like me."

A feeling of fear and dread came over me, and a shiver ran through my entire body.

"How can you talk like that darling? You are only twenty-five years of age."

He looked at me strangely.

"One never knows, Julie. I think I am indestructible, but I could be wrong."

The nurse put her head in the door and quietly reminded Tarek I needed to rest. Off he strode, grinning widely.

I looked up at the ceiling, still emotionally shocked by his words, but later as the nurse brought back my son for his first meal, I pushed them out of my mind.

The five days passed quickly and the day came for my release from the hospital. Tarek, looking casually elegant, arrived promptly, ready and eager to take us both home. Zanab, pert and pretty, had as usual come over and stayed with him, helping with Darren and cooking.

There were many exotic and unusual Arabic names for boys, but after going over so many different ones, I liked only one – Tarek. It was quite common to name a son after his father, so I decided to find out the real translation of the name.

After supper that evening, I questioned Tarek about the meaning of the name in Arabic. He thought for a moment.

"Tarek was a famous Arab warrior. He fought and conquered his way as far as the Rock of Gibraltar, and was feared and well-respected. I like it too, obviously, and it does suit him, if that's what you want."

Looking down at him in my arms greedily feeding, he checked his brown velvet eyes and coal black hair.

"Just the same colour as mine. I think that has evened it up - one for you and one for me." We both laughed and I laid the baby down in his crib next to the bed, and drew him to me.

He kissed me passionately, and our wonder and excitement at the intensity of our love manifested itself over and over again.

With fatherhood this time, I noticed Tarek calmed down a bit, and was showing me in many ways the wonderful, tender, and caring man he could be.

The four of us took many trips together, to outdoor restaurants overlooking flowing streams, to scenic areas around the mountain villages of Bhamdoun and Aley. Tarek Jr. would be snuggled up in a carry-cot in the back seat, and Darren sat up front on my lap.

Every Sunday, we would have lunch with his parents, and this particular balmy day, we decided to drive up in the mountains. We were sitting on the grass, hoards of children of all ages running around us, and I looked up at his strong face, and gazed at his muscular body. Whatever country he was in, Tarek always managed to find a gym to practice his weight-lifting and keep in shape. He shyly told me he had competed in competitions and had the title of "Mr Lebanon", I looked at him shocked. "You never told me that before!"

"You know I am a little embarrassed, and I thought you might not like it" I looked at him lovingly,

" No I am proud of you and how handsome you are, and I love to show you off, and the fact that you keep in such good shape, makes you even more desirable to me my love"!.

The wind started to blow, and we hurriedly gathered up our things, and drove down the winding roads, the famous Cedars of Lebanon trees surrounding us on both sides of the road. Speaking casually, Tarek said

"TMA had another crash last week." I looked up from tending Darren, my face registering shock.

"How does that company continue to operate?" Please look around for some other safely run airline. You know I can work, we would not starve. There are many American and European offices where I could work as a secretary."

He turned, gravely looking at me.

"I couldn't let you work, Julie. People would talk, and say I am unable to support my own wife and would look down on me. It would be humiliating."

I knew it was hopeless to plead more. Nothing was more important than their pride. Looking very serious, Tarek went on.

"I have to stick it out to notch up more flying hours, and then I'll have a chance in another company. But for now, I have a wife and two children, and I cannot leave."

Holding back any further words, knowing I could not change his mind, I clasped his large, strong, tanned hand in silent support.

CHAPTER EIGHTEEN

Tarek, Jr. was nearly three months old, chubby, healthy and contented. Darren was 1 ½ years old, hyper-active and into everything. My husband and I dreamed and talked about taking a trip together, as soon as Tarek Jr. was old enough to be left for a short time. We were planning to fly to Frankfurt and London, taking Darren with us, and were both thrilled at the prospect of the three of us taking a long trip together.

December was still warm, but became crisp and cool in the evenings, with occasional downpours. Christmas was close, and to make extra money, for our upcoming trip, Tarek took a weekend flying trip he was not scheduled for, to Kabul in Afghanistan. I pleaded with him not to go, and told him it was not worth an extra 100 lire, and to please change his mind.

"Please don't go. Let Samir go, he is the one on the roster."

"No, Julie, I must go. We need the extra money."

I could see it was pointless, for some reason, I felt very uneasy about the trip, and could not understand why.

As usual, the company van came around at 10 p.m. and honked its horn. Looking nothing less than superb, hat set at a saucy rakish angle, he kissed me warmly. He ran into the bedroom and gave two big kisses to our sons, and with a last glance around, he bounded down the stairs to the waiting van.

I rushed out to the balcony to wave one last time before he drove off. The door flew open, and he reappeared. He laughed, and explained he had forgotten his watch. One more time, I clung to him asking him over and over again not to go. It wasn't necessary, but he shrugged and left.

I wearily waved again from the balcony until the van was out of sight.

CHAPTER NINETEEN

As was customary on Monday morning, I telephoned TMA operations to check what time Tarek would be arriving from his flight. Their hesitation and uncertainty on the phone worried me, and when they added they did not have any more information at this time, I slammed the phone down in disgust.

To keep from thinking, I busied myself in the house for the rest of the morning, and later in the afternoon, called again. Having learned from experience that being polite and nice was ignored. The next time I called I was very angry, and screaming into the phone, and was eventually put through to an official spokesman. He casually informed me that traffic control had lost contact with the plane.

"Don't worry, I'm sure they landed at another airport", he told me in broken English.

The rest of the evening, I remained frustrated and very restless, and called up a few girlfriends for idle chatter. Hardly sleeping at all that night, as soon as the airline office was open, I began phoning. This went on all day, and still no clue as to where they were, or if they were alright...

The doorbell started ringing and opening it, there stood a very agitated Shariffa and Mahmood. Streams of Arabic spilled out; I could only understand two words out of ten. One of the endless relatives was with them who did speak some English, so he began to patiently translate their outburst. It seems they had been hearing all kinds of different rumours and stories of where the plane was. Crazy, conflicting stories swirled around that it had landed in Russia, and that the plane had been highjacked etc, were just a few of the crazy rumours. It was a complete nightmare. People began ringing the doorbell, with more ridiculous stories, crowds stopping by looking up at the balcony, gesturing and pointing at me etc   I knew then it was time for me to get to the bottom of what had happened to my husband.

I decided to go back to London with Darren, leaving Tarek with my wonderful sister in law Emmina and go to the Russian Embassy there and see what I could find out.

London was dull and depressing. January was one of the worst months, and the freezing cold hit me as I stepped off the plane. Bundled up heavily, we took a taxi to a nearby hotel. The next day, leaving Darren in a competent nearby nursery, I tentatively approached the Russian Embassy.

The officials there were sympathetic and cordial, but refused to substantiate they had seen the plane, or that any of the crew had defected. I knew in my heart it was fruitless, but was willing to try any possibility. I got a lot of publicity in the London Daily Mail and Express and hoped this would help stir up trouble for TMA, as they had an office in the UK and flew in and out of there frequently.. Sadly, knowing I had done as much as I could, I bundled up poor Darren and flew back again to Beirut

I then tackled the TMA office, and creating a stir and disturbance, was at last ushered into the office of one of the Vice-Presidents. Cordially, he ordered coffee for me, and I sat down, seething.

"Mrs. Eddine, we covered a good area around Afghanistan, and spent a lot of money and time on it, and feel this is sufficient."

"Well, I don't think you covered enough of the desolate mountainous areas. These are people's lives you are talking about. They could be stranded somewhere in the middle of nowhere existing on grass and anything else they can find!" I screamed hysterically.

"I know, Mrs. Eddine, this must be very hard on you."

"Hard?!" I screamed. "It's been over a month now, and I don't know whether my husband is dead or alive, and you are talking about how much money it might cost to initiate another search. It's unbelievable!" I got up in a crazy rage, walked out the door, and slammed it shut.

As the days and nights painfully went by I would wake up in bed and feel my love's arms circling my waist. He would stretch, yawn, and we would laugh together over my silly nightmare.

Just as I had predicted, a new search of all the barren and uninhibited areas was undertaken. Still nothing ...

Three months of sheer hell went by, and then the company decided to cut off Tarek's salary. Obviously having no other income, I went out to find a job with one of the many international firms with headquarters in Beirut.

Tarek's parents tried to help, and found a young girl from the mountains to live in so I could go to work each day. This kept me busy throughout the day and stopped me from thinking and going crazy. Girlfriends and Tarek's relatives passed by to comfort and console, but I still felt completely alone and vulnerable in this foreign land with its unknown laws.

All alone, the kids fast asleep, I drank myself into a stupor every night, and as the months wore on, I had no idea if I was a wife or a widow.

His presence was everywhere. All his suits, lotions in the bathroom, and his red silk monogrammed bathrobe still hung in the closet. I buried my face in his clothes, and could still smell his manly scent.

"Oh, what has happened to my love? Has he also been taken from me so young and so cruelly? Would it never end?"

A feeling of complete despair came over me. How I wished I could hear his footsteps outside the door, embrace him again, feel his tanned sinuous body close to mine, and fall passionately onto our favourite couch.

Was this the end of our short and tumultuous love ... was he gone forever?!

Six miserable, unbearable months passed. Joanne, an attractive blond Australian girl, married to a TMA Captain, called me up one day, inviting me over for drinks at her apartment.

The apartment was situated in a high-rise building overlooking the many beautiful beaches in Beirut. She took my hand, and we sauntered onto the balcony, and I looked over at Long Beach, where I had met my love, tears misting my eyes.

"I don't think I will ever see him again in this life", I said, shaking my head in disbelief. "I know him, and if he was alive, he would be back here somehow. I don't know what to think anymore."

Joanne brought two new fresh drinks and put them down on the patio table and was silent. I sipped my drink and made a face.

"Are you trying to make me drunk, Joanne? This is mighty strong."

"Yes, I am afraid I am", she admitted. I looked at her sharply. She had a strange, stricken look on her face.

"I have something here to show you which will come as a great shock to you. That is why I was trying to deaden the pain a little."

"It's about Tarek, isn't it?" I said tremblingly.

"Yes, I'm afraid it is. I'm really sorry, but I have some clothes here you have to identify."

She slowly walked back into the apartment, and as I sat motionless, she reappeared, and raising her hands I could see she was holding a blue sweater – one of Tarek's favourites.

A scream of anguish rushed from my body.

"He's dead, isn't he, Joanne?" She walked over and held me close.

"Yes, his body has been found."

I broke down and sobbed uncontrollably.

She tenderly guided me back into her spare bedroom and told me to lie down.

Giving me time to recover, she sat quietly by the bedside in total support. After awhile, she went on to explain a lone hunter was tracking through the undergrowth in an uninhabited area of Afghanistan. At the foot of a very high mountain, he accidentally came across the plane, and the remains of those on board.

"The bodies have already been flown to Beirut, Julie, and the funeral, I am afraid, has been set for tomorrow." I shot up in the bed.

"Tomorrow? Then the family already knows?"

"Yes, they do. Everyone at TMA thought it would be better coming from another European friend than having some stranger translate this kind of news to you."

"I really appreciate it Joanne, but I cannot face that funeral alone. Would you come with me?"

"I was planning to anyway. You should not have to go through this alone. Let me get us some coffee."

Driving home through the streets, envying the laughing, jostling people, I thought if I could get through this funeral, I could survive anything. A Moslem funeral, I felt would be unlike anything else, and not one I would ever want to repeat.

Emmina, my sweet sister-in-law, eyes wet, and dressed in black, was waiting for me on my doorstep. We held each other close, and she explained in Arabic she would go with me to buy the appropriate clothes for the funeral the next day. In silence, we walked through the crowded souks, and my memories returned to only a few months earlier, walking arm and arm, Tarek and I combed the same souks buying baby clothes. Now, six months later, we were buying black funeral clothes. An appropriate saying came to mind. "God gives with one hand and takes with the other."

Not sleeping at all, I watched the dawn break, and was angry at the clear blue sky of this sad June day. Dressing in my black dress, stocking and veil, I caught a glimpse of myself in the dressing room mirror. I looked with astonishment at my reflection.

"Was this really the happy smiling bride of yesterday? Who was this ashen-faced stranger in black?!!"

Joanne arrived, looking sombre and tense, and drove reluctantly over to the Grandfather's house. Lines of cars and people were waiting in front of the house, and upon catching sight of us, a horrifying screech erupted from the crowd. Darren and Tarek sat in the back looking out of the window, staring wide-eyed and innocently at the staring faces.

The line of cards began the long journey to Harouf in the South of Lebanon, the family's mountain home. In front of our car, the hearse carried a small casket. I looked at it, horrified.

"That couldn't be Tarek, Joanne. He was much bigger than that."

"That is the remains, Julie. You must remember, they were exposed for six months to the elements."

I looked at her, and said no more. What was there to say when you remembered a tall, handsome, beautiful man ... now only remains ...

"I am afraid your Mother-in-law opened up the coffin, because she did not believe it was her beloved son"....I looked at her in shock, 'Oh My God'.?

The next day, after a hot, bumpy ride, we arrived at last in his village Harouf, the place where he was born – a small village, consisting perhaps of 100 people, mostly farmers. A small, quiet, simple village, with no cinemas or public places of any sort. The houses were built lovingly with their own hands, and were constructed out of white quarry brick stone. Acres and acres of vineyards and fruit trees blossomed, and goats, cows, and sheep roamed freely.

On many occasions, Tarek and I had walked together, hand in hand, climbing mountains, picnicking and loving. One particular day, he climbed alone to the top of one very high mountain and screamed his love for me, over and over again. It became music to my ears, as it was re-echoed a thousand times.

As Joanne drove towards the standing line of cars near the burial cemetery, a crowd of people stood in a long line, and at the head of the procession, a young man was holding aloft a blown-up life-size picture of Tarek, in his pilot's uniform. The mourners began to walk towards us, and a hypnotic frenzy began to envelop the crowd. Everyone started screaming, shouting, and wailing, when they reached the car, they began banging on the car, gesturing for us to get out and join the procession.

If my life depended on it at that moment, I could not have moved. They then proceeded to pound on the windows, screaming in Arabic, and I just stared ahead, motionless.

By this time, Joanne was mad. She threw the car door open, and looking extremely dangerous, screamed something unintelligible to them, and the crowd looking at her face, backed away. Jumping back in, she heaved a sigh of relief.

"I was scared out there, but I knew I couldn't show it. You will stay in the car, Julie. They are not sane."

"I don't think I could get out even if I tried. My knees might buckle under me, they're shaking so", I replied quietly. She held my arm tighter, and hushed the boys in the back, who were by now restless and wanted to get out.

We waited silently as the procession walked around the entire village, becoming more and more hysterical. They then all scrambled up the sloping hill towards the cemetery. Looking around, it seemed there were hundreds of people congregated on the hill, all nameless staring faces ... looking at Tarek's blond young Infidel English widow, and their two small children.

It was now time for us to join them, and clutching the boys' hands tightly in mine, I started the long climb. Everyone was watching and waiting for me to collapse. Wrought iron gates were opened, and we stoically walked into the mausoleum.

As we got near the gaping hole, the wailing and moaning reached a peak, and as his body was being lowered into the ground, the two sisters attempted to throw themselves into the hole, clawing out handfuls of their hair by the bloodied roots.

Paralyzed, I stood mute and motionless, not a tear running down my face. Amid more chanting, wailing and shrieks, the earth was finally thrown over the coffin, and stunned and shaking, I stumbled back to the car.

My Arab love had been buried ...and with him, my heart.

CHAPTER TWENTY

From then on, I lived through each day never knowing what shock or surprise awaited me. Working hard all day, it was a pleasure to return to a clean house and a cooked meal. I knew the maid, Fatima, was in collaboration with the Grandparents, and I was sure every move I made was reported to them. They were acting more and more peculiar, and I had no trust in them whatsoever. They were up to something not in my best interest, but what, I did not know.

They dutifully visited many times, and on the surface, they were sweet and caring, but I felt very uneasy. I even became paranoid, and I thought I was being followed. Going shopping one day, I felt eyes boring into my back. Quickly looking back, I saw an old woman run into the nearest shop doorway. For a fleeting second, I thought I recognized her. I was sure she was one of the tenants of the Grandfather's.

I realized soon that I would be penniless. Under Moslem law if the wife was Moslem she inherited 1/6th of the insurance money, a certain percentage went to the parents, and the remainder to the children, if they were boys. A further shock awaited me. Another of the laws from the Koran stated that a non-

Moslem cannot bring up her own children if her husband dies.

Chatting with other friends, they tried to reassure me that everything would be alright. But later, talking with Joanne, she was more realistic and said she was positive that the non-Moslem part would be their ammunition, and they would attack me with this first, and she was sure they would make their move soon.

The following Saturday, the Grandfather appeared at the door, and nervously asked for my Lebanese identity card. Puzzled, I looked at him, and asked in Arabic

"Why do you need it?"

He mumbled something about registering Tarek's death. I went back into the bedroom, and when I came out, made up some excuse that I couldn't find it. He left looking very annoyed.

I ran to the telephone and frantically dialled Joanne's number.

"You had better change your ID to Moslem as soon as possible. You have Protestant on it now, and that would be proof enough for him to take the children away from you. You are a foreigner here, you must protect yourself. You know you don't have any laws protecting you." How well I knew this!!

I hung up the phone in disbelief. Did I have to fight to keep my own children too? It seemed so.

The following evening around 6 p.m., Fatima was putting the children to bed, when the doorbell rang. This time both Grandparents stood at the door, accompanied by Mohammed, one of the relatives who spoke English. I let them in hesitantly. They sat down, and Fatima ran into the kitchen to make coffee.

Mohammed opened up the conversation.

"As you are now a widow, Tarek's parents feel that to keep everything in the family, it would be advisable for you to marry your husband's younger brother, Achmid."

I shook my head in disbelief. Was I hearing right, or was he translating incorrectly?

"But Achmid is only 15!" I said in a shocked voice.

"So! He is old enough, and he would be obliged to marry you for the sake of the family."

I jumped up. "But I don't want to marry a 15 year old boy. It's absolutely impossible!" I screamed.

"Are you sure you will not change your mind?" Mohammed enquired.

"Of course not. It's the craziest thing I have ever heard."

They got up, muttering and talking in fast Arabic and left.

I knew I needed to obtain legal help and counselling. Checking with various friends, Nagib Eli was recommended to me as a lawyer who knew the right people, and usually won cases impossible to others. Contacting him on the phone, I told him of my problem, and he promised to come by the next day, and accompany me to the court to get my religious status changed.

Nagib Eli was a small bony man, black haired and moustached and spoke excellent English, Arabic and French. He drove me downtown to the dilapidated old building and with the usual greetings and pleasantries exchanged, he ushered me in. He took me from one office to another, where I signed various papers connected with my religious status.

Looking around, I was shocked to see Tarek's father standing nearby talking rapidly to one of the Sheikhs. Someone shouted to Nagib from the other side of the courtroom, and looking worried, he walked over to him. Glancing back at the Grandfather, he turned around and anxiously beckoned for me to join him. He pointed at a piece of paper on the desk in front of him, completely in Arabic.

"Does anyone speak English here?" I asked, looking around for Nagib who was out of sight.

"I do", a voice replied at my side.

"What does this mean in English?" I asked, pointing at the paper in front of me.

"Oh it's just a paper to change your religious status to Moslem", a voice replied.

Oh well, just another one like the others. I gaily signed it. In a second, Nagib rushed up to my side.

"What is that you have just signed?!" he screamed. "What did you do?!"

He tore it from the smiling Sheikh and quickly read it. He looked at me seriously.

"You have just signed the paper that you understand your in-laws are taking court proceedings against you to take custody of your children!" He signed.

I looked at him in disbelief. Screaming in the foulest Arabic slang I knew, I ran crying out of the building. Hailing a taxi, I screamed instructions to the taxi driver to take me to Joanne's, and glancing at my angry face, he took off with screeching tires.

Rushing wild-eyed into her apartment, I flung myself on her oval bed.

"You don't have a chance now, Julie! You should get out of the country. You know that if you go to court they will win. You're a foreigner and a non-Moslem."

I knew she was right. Calming down and relaxing, we spent the evening planning an escape route, but after hours of thinking, neither of us came up with a definite plan.

Every day since being tricked by the Grandfather in the courthouse, I packed clothes and personal stuff into either small carrier or shopping bags, and secretly dropped this over at Joanne's apartment. I was sure someone was watching me, and any sign of a suitcase would have immediately alerted the Grandparents of my intentions.

Quietly going to TMA, I was given three tickets for London, and made reservations on a flight leaving on the following Sunday, departing at 11 a.m. from Beirut International. It was imperative to obtain the elusive exit visa from the foreigners municipal building before Sunday, otherwise all was lost. If Tarek's parents were clever, they would have already put our names on the black list at the airport. It was illegal for me to leave, and I knew it, but there was no choice.

Joanne again came to my rescue and she rushed over immediately, and we sat down to plan our strategy. Knowing the Lebanese's weakness for blondes, she told me she intended to flirt and display all her charms to the hilt, and try to captivate them.

My story was my Mother was desperately ill, and I must leave Sunday.

"This is going to be fun. Don't worry, we will get it."

We sped over to the Foreigners' Building, but our luck was out – it was closed. They patiently informed us it would re-open at 7 p.m. At exactly 7 p.m., we were pounding on the door, and at last, a tired-looking guard opened the door. We were ushered into the office of one of the officials and sat down. He greeted us with typical warm hospitality.

Looking very upset and distraught, I spoke.

"Mr. Khoury, my mother is very sick and I need an exit visa, so I can leave on Sunday morning."

He leaned back in his chair, looked appreciatively at Joanne dressed in a skin-tight sweater and short skirt and ordered coffee and cold drinks. He began asking us about our backgrounds, and enquired how we liked Beirut, etc. and quite obviously wanted this tete-a-tete to continue a long time.

Joanne edged her skirt a little higher and leaned a little closer to him, and I soon noticed tiny beads of sweat breaking out on his upper lip. They both laughed and chatted together, but keeping to my role, I appeared worried and subdued. After about half an hour of this, he pushed his chair back and got to his feet.

"I'm afraid I cannot give you the visa myself, but my colleague, Hassan Diab can and he will be here shortly."

Joanne looked mad. Had she wasted all her charms on an underling?!!

Throughout the interview, I kept gazing fascinated at a large manila folder on his desk. On the label, clearly marked was my name. Checking it once, I felt sure he would see a copy of the court case pending against me, and all pertinent facts on my family history.

In a few moments, Hassan Diab returned. Mr. Khoury, taking my passport with him, went into his office and closed the door. I looked at Joanne in fear, both of us with our fingers crossed. A couple of minutes passed, and then Mr. Khoury returned, my passport in his hand.

"Do have a nice visit, Mrs. Eddine. I do hope your Mother recovers."

"Thank you very much", I said in a subdued voice.

We walked gravely out, and Joanne had a secret smile of success on her face. I felt sure, without her keeping him so busy flirting, he would have opened up the manila folder.

Away from the grim building, I gave her a hug.

"I knew you would do it."

A couple I knew before in England were staying with me, and they promised to help me out with my plan.

The Grandparents always came to visit on Sunday mornings about 10 a.m., and I persuaded my friends to keep them talking as long as they could to enable us to leave the country before they suspected anything.

CHAPTER TWENTY~ONE

Tossing and turning all night, the fateful day of departure arrived. Looking out of the window, I cursed the fact it was such a great sunny day, perfect for the beach where I would have preferred to be, instead of going to England. Packing a few last minute things in plastic bags, I looked around and tried to imprint it all in my memory. One last time, I turned and saw my personal pictures and sentimental gifts Tarek brought me from all around the world. All these treasures had to be left behind. Shutting the door, I checked for spies, and holding tightly onto the boys' hands, hailed a passing cab.

I hurried over to Joanne's, looking back fearfully through the rear window for any followers. Riding up in the lift to the 11th floor, the gates to her apartment were already opened by a very anxious lady.

Joanne looked at me in alarm.

"I was so worried you were not going to make it, it's getting late." She opened her door and pushed us through. Without hesitating, I ran out to the balcony and took one last look at the breathtaking view, and stared for the last time at my beach of destiny.

Picking up my few belongings, we hailed a cab outside and soon arrived at the airport. Feeling like a fugitive fleeing from justice, I anxiously looked around for any vaguely familiar faces who would recognize us.

Finding a secluded corner of the large airport, we sat down and waited for the announcement to go downstairs. The first call came over the loudspeaker, and embracing my dear friend, the boys and I walked slowly towards the passport official at the barrier line. Striding up to the young Lebanese, he checked my passport for the exit visa, casually glanced at the children, and waved us on. I walked briskly away, expecting any second to be called back.

Hiding out in the ladies' room, I stayed there as long as possible, waiting for the final call to board the aircraft. It seemed forever, but at last I heard our flight number, called the children to my side, and with trembling legs, walked towards the plane.

I did not breathe evenly until I heard the engines purr. As the plane began to ascend into the air, I looked back, still expecting to see Shariffa running down the tarmac towards the plane, white headdress trailing behind, and Mahmood with hoards of gesturing, screaming, nameless relatives running down the tarmac towards me...

After the tedious long flight, trying valiantly to stop two energetic children from playing tag in the aisle, I arrived in London, exhausted. The weather was arm and balmy, and a welcome change from my last winter visit.

Finding a phone at the airport, I dialled my Step-Grandmother's number. Her opening remarks were not encouraging.

"What on earth are you doing here, Julie?"

I tried to explain to her about the court case and the Grandparents, but it seemed to fall on deaf ears. I could already sense that she thought I was going to be some sort of burden to her, especially with two small children. Her voice became hesitant.

"We tried to contact you in Beirut to inform you that your father passed away last week." What? Another death, another shock – would they never end?

"What happened? How did he die?" I asked.

"He was found in his rooming house dead in bed", she answered coolly. "We attended the funeral a couple of days ago. Your brother is still here and arranged everything."

Words were inadequate, as I said nothing. There was no instant invitation from her, so I hesitantly asked if we could stay there temporarily, until I could find somewhere else. She reluctantly agreed, and feeling like a condemned prisoner, I found the underground station and stepped out at Paddington station.

Looking out of the compartment window at the contrasting colours and beautiful scenery with cows and sheep grazing so peacefully, my mind raced back to thoughts of my black-haired handsome father. He had been riding on the top of the waves for so long, and a few years ago, came crashing down. At the top of his profession, he married a beautiful widow who gave birth to five sons in quick succession. He then developed an insane jealousy over her imagined lovers, had a mental breakdown, and she finally divorced him. So sad, his final breath taken in some obscure furnished room, alone, leaving behind 6 sons and one daughter.

It seemed as if the train purposely stopped at every station, but I didn't care. I was not in a particular rush to get there anyway.

The next few weeks were a constant nervous strain. My Step-Grandmother (my aunt as she liked to be called) was constantly on the watch all the time for the slightest dirty hand marks the children made, and my welcome was definitely running out.

A few days later, I visited my Auntie Dolly's house, my mother's sister, and my brother was there. I waited anxiously for an invitation to stay with him for a short time, but nothing. No word of sympathy on my loss, only grumbles and complaints he had to arrange the funeral on his own, and pay the expenses. In fact what he was saying was, "You have made your bed lie in it"...wonderful

I lost my temper, blew up, and stormed out of the house, vowing never to have anything more to do with my brother David, again.

Walking the streets looking for accommodation, at last I found a one bedroom apartment in a rotten old house up three flights of stairs, with the toilet one flight below. It was bad, but it was the only thing I could find centrally situated, near available work. I had no furniture, but was able to buy some second-hand stuff. My doubts were returning every hour about returning back to England, but where else could I have gone?

An application was made at a nearby local nursery school, and the hunt was on for employment. Washing nappies in the sink, and hanging them out to dry in the garden as I had before did not work, and there were no Laundromats nearby. At last, a vacancy was found in the nursery school, and I pushed Darren and Tarek eight blocks in the pram to drop them off.

Soon I found a job with an employer who was willing to take a chance on a woman with two small children. Winter was approaching, and it was a gruelling time, and as I trudged through the snow each morning pushing the pram, I cursed my restless nature, and its dire eventual consequences.

I returned to the depressing apartment, frozen and weary, and facing me would be the unwashed dirty nappies, dirty dishes, and unmade beds. How long could I take this, I wondered? Looking around with distaste at my surroundings, I noticed the fresh hole in the window of the bedroom. The stuffed paper did not stop the draft, and freezing cold was still seeping through. The oil heaters were not sufficient to warm the room, and the coal downstairs was just too heavy for me to carry up three flights. This was only temporary, I knew from this point on, there was only one way to go and that was up, and I felt confident something soon would change.

Loathing this cold with a passion, I again cursed ever seeing the sandy beaches of Beirut, and the sparkling blue Mediterranean Sea. Had I never seen it, I would not know what I was missing.

It was rare I could spend an evening out of the house. First, I could not leave the children alone, and secondly, I could not afford a babysitter. An old friend of my mother's son did come over very occasionally and babysat for me to give me a chance to leave the depressing apartment.

Making an appointment with the local doctor, I asked immediately for a prescription for the pill. He brusquely asked me my marital status, and upon learning I was a widow, turned me down, without further explanation, old fashioned hypocrites.

Naturally, being young and healthy, I was missing sex, and was a prime target for one-night stands. The whole combination of the environment, climate and my feeling of complete helplessness over my situation was driving me wild.

A few months later, I realized I was pregnant. What on earth would I do now?

There was absolutely nobody to turn to, and I seriously contemplated suicide, but looking at my innocent boys relying on me for their meagre existence, I changed my mind. Where could I get an abortion? I could not have another child. I could hardly handle two alone, let alone three. Abortion was illegal, and the only recourse would be a back-street type of abortion, where so many girls before me had already been butchered and died as a result.

How ironic ... perhaps fate... a generation later, I was now in a similar situation as my mother ... Was I destined to die in the same way?

Asking around secretly, I found someone who knew someone. The horrible evening arrived – I was now five months pregnant – I was flirting with death. The doorbell rang. I opened it nervously, and in walked a small mousy-haired middle-aged housewife. Could this be her?

"Are you the lady with the room for rent?" This had been our pre-conceived password.

I numbly nodded, and looking around her suspiciously, walked quickly into the room and shut the door. Checking the various rooms, she immediately asked or the money, and hurriedly stuffed it into her worn-out pockets. Trembling visibly, she tried to reassure me and then asked me to take off my clothes. She went into the kitchen, and returned with a douche.

"Are you ready?" Would anyone be ready for anything like this, I thought

A violent pain engulfed me. She jumped up, told me to call the hospital immediately, and ran out of the door in a panic.

Ignorant as I was, I thought I could handle this myself at home, and never thought I would have to go to the hospital. Hobbling downstairs, I banged on the door of the young couple below me. I tried to explain to them, between spasms of excruciating pain, I was going to the hospital, and please call someone to take care of my boys. Looking at me wide-eyed, I hobbled back upstairs, doubled over in agony. Managing to call the ambulance, at last I heard the sirens getting nearer and nearer. Would they ever get here?

At last, someone knocked on my door, and immediately laid me on a stretcher. Moaning and groaning from the pain, I never imagined it could ever be this painful. With sirens screaming, we arrived at the emergency room. Agonizing hours later, and unable to comprehend this whole mass of pain engulfing my body, my baby was born dead. I could not look, or question its sex. I was too upset to think or speak. I was a murderess!

Lying for many hours in the hospital bed gave me lots of time to think about my situation and realize I had to change it. It was impossible to continue as I was, completely alone with two small babies, and I made the decision to return to Beirut, to try somehow to sort the problem out.

After five days, against the doctor's orders, I rushed over to the address where my sons were staying. They rushed into my arms so innocently.

The only person I could think of who would or could take care of the boys while I made my trip to Beirut was my cousin Anne. She was the only understanding, caring relative I possessed, and even though she had three children of her own, I knew she would not hesitate to help. I was right.

"Of course, what is two more?" she replied.

She lived in Ilminster, a pretty country town in Devizes, and was one of the best mothers I knew to leave them with. Packing up a couple of suitcases, I arrived with Daren and Tarek, and she was there to welcome us at the station. Clutching her to me, I felt her warmth and support.

"Don't worry Julie. I will take good care of them while you are in Beirut."

CHAPTER TWENTY~TWO

The next morning, bright and early, hugging my boys close, I took the train back to Bristol, I had already obtained the ticket from TMA, and it was waiting for me at the airport.

Circling over Beirut again, and making a perfect landing, I walked happily through Customs and Immigration.

I felt home again, and realized how much this city meant to me.

Someone knocked me on the shoulder, and turning my head, I stopped dead in my tracks, as a young handsome pilot dressed in a TMA uniform casually brushed past me. I looked back at him, and my heart fluttered – what cruelty!

Stamping my passport, the official hurried me on. Through the panelled-off glass of the visitors' section, I spied my old reliable friend Joanne waiting impatiently for me. As soon as the Custom Officer stamped his chalked sign on my suitcase, she ran up to me.

"I am so pleased to see you, Julie. You cannot imagine the goings-on, after you escaped."

I hugged her and we went outside to hail a cab.

The palm tree-lined boulevards, honking cards and bewildering traffic all looked the same, nothing had changed. Later in the evening, lounging on her balcony overlooking the same blue Mediterranean, I looked longingly at the beach. I shook my head in bewilderment.

"Joanne, little did I know when I looked into those dark eyes, the heartache ahead of me. Do you think it would have made any difference, had I known?"

She brought some fresh fruit to the table.

"No Julie, to be honest, I don't think anything would have stopped you." I laughed.

"You might be right, Joanne. Sit down and tell me what has been going on since I left."

"Well, I don't know where to start. Okay, let's begin with what happened when Tarek's parents found out you really left the country. Oh my!" She picked up a cluster of grapes and began eating them one by one. She rattled on.

"They first of all did not believe you left the country, and got the police and search parties combing the whole of Beirut, including the mountains. You were a wanted fugitive from justice, Julie." And she peeled with laughter.

"After this was unsuccessful, they came to their senses, and went to the airport. Of course, they found your name there and went mad. They all tore off to the Securities of Foreigners in fleets of cars, and physically attacked that poor man, whatever his name. Anyway, I have forgotten."

"Physically attacked him?" I asked, shocked.

"Yes, I think he landed up in the hospital. They were so mad at him for not checking the manila folder, because inside there was a copy of the court case. He was kind of lax. I wonder why?" We screamed with laughter.

"Anyway, after that, I believe the Grandfather drove over to the apartment with a truck and took everything out, and an official seal was put on the door. That's all I know."

The phone began to ring, and Joanne ran back inside.

I could just imagine the scene, and would have hated to be the person they were angry with, and hoped by now they had calmed down, but I doubted it.

I looked around me, the lights were twinkling from the high-rises nearby, and you could smell the sea, and see the rippling movements of the waves crashing onto the shore. Tears started to stream down my face, everything seemed so unfair, but life was – I knew this many years ago.

Joanne reappeared with shrimp hors d'oeuvres and more chilled wine and we sat contentedly on the balcony, enjoying the tranquility and beauty of Beirut by night.

Opening up the window the next morning, I could see it was going to be a beautiful sun-drenched day. I dressed quickly and padded to the kitchen, and Joanne and I sipped on fresh-squeezed orange juice, and ate a leisurely breakfast on the balcony.

Calling on the phone, I was able to locate my old lawyer, Nagib Eli. Surprised, but pleased at my return, I informed him of my situation and told him I wished to negotiate some kind of agreement.

"Nagib, I also need a Moslem lawyer, just to make sure this does not turn into a religious battle"?

He agreed that this was a good idea, and recommended Mustapha Riad, who was well known and respected in religious circles. We made arrangements to gather in his office the next morning, and he promised he would call Shariffa and Mahmoud and get everything fixed up.

Later that evening, Joanne and I walked to the nearest restaurant overlooking the Pigeon Rock. This was one of the many restaurants perched on the rocks, with a beautiful view of the sea.

Joanne was dressed in a blue silk pantsuit, and I borrowed one of her pink sundresses, as my wardrobe now was sparse. We sat sipping champagne, looking at the moon and watching the twinkling lights from distant boats. Suddenly, someone tapped me on the shoulder. I whirled around. There standing in all her glory, stood Lila, with a beaming Omar looking on. We both embraced.

"What on earth?"

"We could say the same thing", Lila said.

"Please sit down, both of you. I don't know what to say, this is a real shock."

I introduced them both to Joanne, but before I could even get her name out properly, I could see Lila could not be shut up, and before another word was said, burst out, "Omar and I are married."

"You are what?? That's marvellous, but how?"

Her happiness was contagious, and her words tumbled over each other in their intensity. She told us Rashid died suddenly over a year ago from another heart attack. They were now able to admit their love

117

for each other and marry, as they should have years ago. I was so happy for her, I could not speak.

She looked at me strangely.

"What happened to you? Where's your husband?"

Overwhelmed and emotionally drained, I jumped out of my seat, and rushed out to the bathroom. A few minutes later, Joanne came in. Standing firmly, hands on hips, she looked at me sternly.

"You cannot escape the truth. You have to accept he is dead, and you have to go on living. Now come back and join your friends, I have told them everything." I thanked her and returned to the table.

Omar and Lila were sympathetic and understanding, and we spent a delightful evening, which passed too quickly. We spent the rest of the evening in sweet remembrances of Cairo, and my first glimpse of Lila's belly dancing in "Sahara City". They were returning back to Cairo the next day, and looking at them so much in love, I felt the old ache return for my lost love, and felt horribly cheated.

Joanne got up suddenly.

It's time, we really should be going. I have told Omar and Lila you have a big day tomorrow."

Tearful goodbyes were exchanged, and both of us swearing on a lifelong friendship and communication, Joanne and I left.

Arriving at the lawyer's office the following day, I waited nervously for their arrival. Would they curse me, kill me, what? I did not know! Stories from other friends warned me that Ali, the eldest brother, had vowed to kill me on sight. I hoped he was not coming with them, gun in hand.

Mustapha and Eli were there looking calm and competent. The mumble of Arabic voices came closer and they burst into the room, their lawyer in tow. Looking at me with hate, they rattled off a stream of Arabic curses. The air was tense, and the two lawyers stared at my in-laws' lawyer with distrust.

Eli looked at me and quietly said:

"Just speak up and tell the lawyer what you want, and what would satisfy you to return to Lebanon with the children."

Their lawyer, staring at me with lustful eyes, looked at me challengingly.

"I don't want any money. The best thing to do would be to put all the insurance money together and buy an apartment here, to be bought in the children's name. I also will not tolerate any interference from Tarek's parents in my private life. The court case will, of course, have to be withdrawn, and if all these demands are agreed to, I will return to Beirut with the children." I sat down breathless.

There was an eerie silence, and then their Moslem lawyer translated my statements into Arabic.

More loud Arabic took place, mostly from my Mother-in-law. He told me this was agreeable to a certain extent, but it would take time to convince them of it all. I knew that endless arguing back and forth would go on for hours, and was prepared for it.

"Also, please tell them that when we do buy the apartment, we live in it or rent it out to help with the boys' education. I don't want them going to the free schools."

As this was translated, a piercing scream sounded from Shariffa, and she stood up, my black-haired, strong-looking Mother-in-law, swathed in her white Mecca headdress. He translated to me that the mother said what had been good enough for her son, would be good enough for her son's sons.

Standing up to my full 5'7", I screamed back.

"They will go to a decent school, where they can be taught English, to help their future", and sat down.

This was again translated, and as she rose to strike me, the Grandfather restrained her. Drawing Mustapha closer to me, I asked him what happens if I ever wanted to get married again? Mustapha raised his eyebrows as if to say 'You are really pushing your luck.'!!

In a few minutes, he spoke rapidly to their lawyer. Another piercing scream from the grandmother, and she stood up and marched out the door. The lawyer ran after her, and in a few minutes, brought her back, still screaming and cursing. The Grandfather tried in vain to calm her down, and after about ten minutes, she eventually sat down.

I knew then it would be impossible ever to marry here again, but at the moment, it was still better than the life I was living in England.

I looked around at the assortment of strange people sitting around in the office. It was a bizarre comedy scene... How had I managed to arrive in this situation? At least now, I knew I would have a decent place to live, a maid, and also be able to find a job in one of the many European firms.

The conversations in Arabic and English continued, and eventually the terms of the contract were set out.

I would receive nothing from the insurance money, nor would the Grandparents.

The money would be put into an apartment, to be bought in the children's names, both parties in mutual agreement on the location.

The Grandfather would be named as a guardian with me.

The court case against me had been withdrawn.

They would not interfere in my private and personal life.

The last one, I knew, was a real break-through. It was extremely difficult for them not to interfere, but they had signed a warrant for my eventual departure from the country, when they were forbidding me to marry. I was content to stay here now until the children were older, but regarded this as a temporary refuge and residence until that time.

The next few days were spent enjoying the climate and beaches of Beirut, and also experiencing again the hospitality, which is unsurpassed in the world. I rested and relaxed for the first time in a very long and hard year, and basked in the sun, the sea and the atmosphere. All the Lebanese I met were fun-loving people, and seemed uninterested in wars and fighting.

The atmospheres and cultures of the old and new give off a rare mixture of exotic fragrances that is unique. Beirut has a large population of Armenians who came as refugees from Turkey, escaping from the Turkish massacre and with the thousands of

Europeans, Americans, and Lebanese; it was a mixed and interesting population.

As the French occupied Lebanon for so many years, the driving is easily recognizable as driving in Paris. It is chaotic and fast, and very few rules or regulations are followed. After seeing many an unsuspecting European emerge from a taxi cab, ashen-faced and shaking, I knew they had just experienced a few close crashes, sudden screaming tire stops, and red lights that were completely ignored!

The Lebanese Government consists of the most unusual variety of religions in the world. The President is always Christian Maronite, the Prime Minister Moslem Sunni, and the Speaker of the House, Moslem Shia. This way, most of the religious denominations are represented. The Drews, another religious order, is so unusual that according to their own law, they cannot be told about their beliefs until they are 40. Every resident has an official identification card, and on this card, your religious beliefs are prominently displayed.

My days of relaxation came to an end, and Joanne knew it was soon time for me to leave to pick up the boys. I again said my farewell, this time only for a short time, and winged my way back to London, and the inevitable train ride to Bristol, and on to the contrasting countryside of Ilminster. I was so happy to see my children, and embraced them once more.

Anne, looking bright and cheery, was a little dubious about the marriage bit when I told her the conditions of the contract. I thanked her and thanked her for saving my life, and again flew back to Beirut, the kids excited to be leaving the cold weather behind.

CHAPTER TWENTY-THREE

Going back to the old in-laws house and staying there with the two kids was very scary, what if they had reopened the case and would grab them from me again?

Locating a suitable apartment, agreeable to everyone, was a harder chore than I imagined. They wanted it, of course, in a strictly Moslem area, whereas I wanted it in a more mixed or European area. Just to escape from the chaotic house, and hordes of relatives, I agreed to an apartment in a nice new building, too close for my comfort to their area.

Calling Joanne, I invited her to come with me and look it over. We wandered through, and checked the three bedrooms, dining room, sitting room, and walked out onto the long balcony.

"It looks fine, Julie. At least you're not far from me in a cab."

Through some friends of Joanne, I found a new maid named Faruz. She was young, pretty and trustworthy, and was thrilled to be working for a European, and grateful to be away from her village, and in the big city. She knew she would be treated as one of the family, and given plenty of time off.

I found a job with an American company, Abbott Laboratories, and went back to work, leaving a very competent and reliable Faruz in charge.

My new social life began.

Samir Sobrani had been a close pilot friend of Tarek's, and was devastated about his death. He was the one chosen for the ill-fated flight, but it was Tarek who insisted on taking it over for the extra money. During his disappearance and funeral, Samir showed concern, sympathy and support. He was a stocky, curly black-haired man, kind and generous, and we began going out together. As our dates and meetings continued, I began to suspect he was more serious than I, and was definitely thinking of marriage. Samir was delightful, but I knew my limits, and knew the result and outcome of any marriage in Lebanon, so I tried to discourage him.

"Samir, you know that Shariffa and Mahmoud would never agree to anything between you and I." He looked at me shocked.

"But why, Julie? I am Moslem too, why would they object?"

"I know them pretty well now Samir, they would not care what you were, they would just be able to take the children by their own law."

He took me in his arms.

"I care about you Julie. You know that. Why do they have to make our life difficult?"

I realized he would never understand, and it was up to me not to spend so much time with him.

As the months passed, it became more and more difficult for me to have any privacy or freedom. Every time I would leave the apartment, nosy neighbours above would be leaning over the balcony staring, and sometimes one of them would come up to the car, and rudely peer and leer in. Things grew worse and worse. They considered me an immoral woman for dating, and slang Arabic curses were screamed at me as I would leave the building. Some even attempted to throw stuff down from the balcony in an attempt to hit me. It was time to start checking around for another place to live.

That weekend, Tarek Jr., Darren and I set out for the day to a new beach named "Tabarja". Lying sunning myself, I needed to cool down, and ran headlong into the wavy water. After a long and relaxing swim, I walked up the beach slowly, and looking around for Darren and Tarek, I saw them playing sand castles with a small blond-haired, blue-eyed little girl. Walking towards them, I noticed a lady advancing on the little girl and talking to her rapidly. As I approached, I immediately knew this was her mother, blond and blue-eyed like her daughter and immediately recognized a British accent. I introduced myself, and she invited me to join her, and her daughter Tracey. Finding out her name was Valerie, we spent the whole afternoon talking and exchanging backgrounds and stories of England, and I knew here was a real close friend. Plans were already made for a house-warming party the following Saturday, so of course, I invited my new-found friend.

Faruz was thrilled at the prospect of a party, and spent all day in the kitchen, cooking and re-arranging the furniture. I dressed in a silver sequined pant outfit, and was looking forward to some company for the first time in my apartment. Joanne, Valerie, Mohammed,

Samir, and many others arrived, and everyone seemed to have a great time. At last, at 2 a.m., I thankfully closed the door on my last guest.

Rushing back from work the next evening, Faruz, in an anxious voice, called me into the kitchen.

"It seems all the gossip mongers in the building have told everyone around we all had a sex orgy here last night."

"A what?" I exclaimed.

"They also said I was involved in it, and they called the Vice Squad."

She giggled hysterically.

I sighed. This was too much – I just had to find another area to live. I would not live anymore with this mentality. That evening, the doorbell rang, and there stood a very embarrassed Vice Squad Officer. I invited him in. He apologized and told me he was obliged to investigate any call he receives. He sat down.

"They are extremely jealous of you because being the only widow or single person in the building, you can come and go as you please. They also check on the TV repairman or plumber to see how long he stays, thinking you are paying them with sexual favours." I shook my head in disbelief, but knew he was telling me the truth.

The following day, I passed by my in-laws and informed them we would be leaving the apartment soon, and would be looking in a different area. As per our agreement, I reminded them the rent money could be used for school and expenses for the children.

I soon found a nice, spacious apartment in a completely different area, right next door to the British

Ambassador's residence. We moved in, and I noticed many foreigners coming and going from the apartment, and felt much more comfortable, and at ease.

Samir started to become too intense and jealous, and I knew a final confrontation would soon take place between him and Tarek's parents. It wasn't long.

The next weekend, plans had been made to go to the mountains skiing, and we intended to stay until Sunday night. The mountain resorts are numerous, and most weekends, you could find many Lebanese and foreigners enjoying the sun, slopes and snow. The boys just loved to race down the slopes in sledges, and learned fast how to ski, as being so young, there was no fear and they learned fast. The blue skies above, combined with the white snow, and the crisp clean air, gave us rosy cheeks, and a hearty appetite. The hotels were modern and well equipped, and the weekend was over too soon. Driving down the mountains, I looked tenderly at Samir. He was a wonderful kind man, but there was not that deep sexual sensation or safeness I felt with Tarek, and anyway, there was too much to lose in marrying anyone.

We eventually drove up to the apartment, tired and dishevelled, and waiting outside the front door, looking extremely angry, was the famous pair. Immediately on sight, Lila began screaming at Samir. I just stood by and waited, catching a few words here and there. He reacted well – cool and polite.

"What did they say?" I asked after they both left.

"They said they were worried about the children's safety, and didn't want us taking them to dangerous places."

"That's ridiculous, skiing is not dangerous, it's a popular sport." I replied, taking off the boys' heavy ski jackets.

He sat down, looking at me seriously.

"You might as well know, I have already told them I want to marry you."

"What? Oh no, you haven't! No wonder they were waiting for us."

"I'm afraid you're right, Julie. They told me they would come and take Darren and Tarek away, even if it was me." I nodded my head.

"I did warn you, Samir, that they would. There is no future for us, they would make our life hell, and I would lose the boys, and that is something I never intend to do."

He left looking rejected and forlorn, and I knew our relationship was doomed. I slowly backed away from him and began dating on a non-serious basis, enjoying other friends, and my new freedom.

CHAPTER TWENTY~FOUR

The next year, the five-day war with Israel began. Curfew was mandatory, and all headlights on cars and in buildings had to be covered or extinguished. We crept around with candles, and passed the time watching old re-runs, and playing cards.

A strange atmosphere came over the city, and people scurried around, just hoping to get from one place to another in one piece. One day, walking to the nearest grocery store for some emergency food, a squadron of screaming jets flew overhead. Instinctively, I ducked and hid and watched with fear. Without warning, the jets dived towards Beirut, swooping down, practically hitting the highest building, and just as suddenly, ascended up again. This happened two or three times a day and nobody was ever sure if any bombs were ever going to be released from these planes.

The Lebanese still tried to continue to enjoy themselves, regardless of the curfew. One evening, a crowd of us spent the whole night in a local night club named "Caves du Roy" this was in a basement and was a popular nightclub, full of intriguing statues, live bands, interesting people and fun. At 4 a.m. in the morning, curfew was over and everyone went home, so I was only able to sleep a couple of hours before returning to work. One particular night walking up the stairs to leave, I was pinched, looking shocked, I looked up into the face of the famous actor Omar Sharif looking as handsome as ever... with his velvet eyes and long eyelashes, another reminder of my Arab love..he winked and laughed and went on down!

A few more months went by, and I really thought things were getting back to normal when curfew was lifted. The next week, however, driving from the local cinema with Valerie, Tracey and the boys, I was astounded to see tanks stationed around town. What was going on now?

A young American girl, Sue, studying at the American University of Beirut, was staying with me, and had been for the last six months. It was fun having her around, and the boys loved her. Returning from school one day, she dashed into my room, looking extremely upset.

"I have to leave, the American Embassy has said it's not safe here, and Pan American Airways are coming to pick us up and take us home. I don't want to go." And she let out a hysterical laugh.

I ran to her and held her close as the tears were now beginning to fall.

"Do you think I will ever be able to come back? I love it here so."

"I don't know, Sue, it's hard to say. The British Embassy hasn't told us to leave yet, but you know the British are always the last to go. She managed to force a small laugh, and went back into her bedroom to pack.

"I am supposed to be at the airport at 8 p.m. this evening, it's awful." She screamed from the bedroom.

I sadly put her few belongings into my little red MG, and took off for the airport. Security jeeps and road blocks seemed everywhere. We were stopped three or four times and asked to show identification, and I was nervous. Gunfire could be heard in the background, and turning to look at Sue, she looked so sad, so was oblivious to her surroundings.

At last we arrived at the airport, and I could see the Pan American jets gleaming in the sun. As we swung up to the entrance, I noticed a large crowd of Americans, with just a handful of luggage, standing around looking mystified, scared, and helpless. I parked the car, and walked with Sue into the airport.

A special area had been cordoned off for the Americans told to leave. She embraced me warmly, jotted down her address in America, and joining her compatriots, she walked reluctantly towards the waiting planes.

Waving sadly, I doubted I would ever see her again.

I carefully drove back to the apartment, and again noticed the ominous-looking tanks stationed at various street crossings. As I walked into the foyer of the building, Faruz and the kids rushed out, afraid that something terrible had befallen me.

This was my first warning; I should be looking for a safer country to live.

CHAPTER TWENTY~FIVE

The skirmishes between the rival religious factions came to an end, and everything appeared normal once more.

The conflicts were between the Christian-backed militia and the Moslem-backed militia over the ratio of power held by the Christians and the Moslems. The Moslems, although having the population majority in the country, had less power than the Christians, and the endless battles and disputes depended on the power being evenly distributed in the government jobs, the armed forces, police and the special secret police force.

I began thinking about my close friend, Jennie, who had stayed with me last year in my apartment on Cornich Mezra. I had been introduced to her by some friends working in the British Embassy. She was English, but worked and lived in Australia, and raved about the country, its friendly people, and the wonderful climate, and had begged me to come and visit her. Letter upon letter had arrived inviting me to Sydney, and she promised she would obtain a job for me with the company she worked for.

In various conversations with other Australians living here, I was told it was a new, large and exciting country, who needed immigrants. Perhaps I should go and see, and find out for myself. Luckily, I was still entitled to receive reduced tickets from TMA, so I made the decision to go.

Calling Valerie on the phone to check if she was home, I jumped into my little red car, and sped over to her apartment to talk it over with her.

Stepping into the lift, my thoughts returned to a cloudy rainy Sunday in March of last year. Faruz had left for the mountains for her weekend off, and the children were playing cowboys and Indians, but even with that noise going on, there was no stirring from Jennie's bedroom. It was past 12:00, and I began to get a little concerned.

She had been depressed lately over a local boyfriend, Shahada. Jennie was a tall, good-looking, black-haired elegant lady. She worked for a conglomerate of magazine publishers in Sydney, and travelled extensively for them. On her many trips to Beirut on business, she met and eventually fell in love with Shahada, and was waiting for a serious commitment from him. I knew it was hopeless, as she told me his parents told him to forget her, as they had picked someone very suitable for him from their village.

I knocked tentatively on her door, and opened it part way. "Jennie, are you up?" Dead silence. I pushed open the door a little further. I saw her lying in a comatose position, white as a sheet. I rushed over – her breathing was very laboured. Looking around, I immediately noticed empty pill bottles strewn around the room.

"Oh my God, what has she done?" I thought.

I slapped her face a couple of times and shook her, but it was like trying to shake a corpse.

I ran to the telephone, and called my own doctor, who was also a personal friend and confidante.

"Dr. Haddad, I think my girlfriend, Jennie has tried to commit suicide. Can you come quickly?"

"Julie, please check the name of the drug on the empty bottles, and let me know what she has taken." I madly dashed into the bedroom, and gave him the information.

"Listen, Julie, this has to be handled very privately and discreetly. Here in Lebanon, if someone tries to commit suicide, and if the authorities find out, they will deport her, and she can never return. This is the reason she cannot go to the hospital."

"Oh, I didn't know that", I replied, shocked. "You are right, she would be devastated if she was forced to leave and could not return. What can I do now?"

"As its Sunday, it's going to be difficult. You have to go to the Pharmacy and buy the IV equipment to fix up over her bed. Also, you need to locate a nurse to constantly monitor her breathing and recovery. I will be over in a minute to give her an injection and check her out. I'm on my way." I hung up the phone with relief.

Leaving the door ajar for the doctor, I ran to the nearest Pharmacy, and managed to buy all the equipment Dr. Haddad requested. Rushing back inside, I found him already examining her, shaking his head.

"It doesn't look good. I have just given her an injection which I hope increases her heartbeat, because it's awfully weak."

Suddenly, the door flew open and the two children rushed in.

"What's wrong with Jennie?" Tarek asked.

"Oh, she's just sick boys; now go out onto the balcony and play. The doctor is going to help her."

Dr. Hassad looked at me, looking grim.

"Were you able to find a nurse to keep an eye on her?" Before I could reply, he interrupted me.

"Let me think ... I must know someone myself, but it must come from you, I cannot be involved. My license is at stake here."

He rapidly wrote down a number on a scrap of paper, and gathering up his stethoscope and bag, he walked towards the door.

"This is all I can do to help, Julie. The syringe must be kept in her wrist until she recovers, if she does. I think the injection might have saved her."

He ran down the stairs.

Quickly dialling the number of the nurse, I rattled off the address, and she promised she would be there shortly. Heaving a sigh of relief, I sat down. This was something I had not expected.

Two anxious days passed, and then on the third day, Jennie's eyes fluttered open. Oh, what a relief I felt. She was going to make it. Shahada phoned and I told him the bad news. That evening he visited her, acting very casual and unconcerned, and my heart ached for poor Jennie. A couple of months later, Jennie left and returned to Sydney, realizing the futility of her love.

135

All these flashback memories still whirling around in my brain, I realized that the lift had already stopped at Valerie's floor. Later, sipping on some good English tea, Valerie thought the trip was a good idea, knowing that Jennie was already there as a friend and supporter.

"Listen, Julie, I will take care of the boys for you, so you won't have to worry about them." I looked at her in astonishment – what a friend she was.

"In fact, the lease on this place is up soon, as you know, and with Ralph in Saudi Arabia, it would be better for you if Tracey and I just move into your place, so that when you return you will still have a home. How does that sound?"

It sounded perfect to me.

The Pan American flight took off from Beirut, and checking the passengers, I could see there was more crew than passengers. The trip was unbelievably long. I really thought I would be flying for the rest of my life.

At last, the stewardess announced we were approaching Hong Kong. At least I could spend a few hours in the exciting city, stretch my legs and get out of this plane at last.

The atmosphere of the East and West cultures was fascinating and taking a harbour ferry across to the other island of Hong Kong, the scenery was exciting and different. Time passed so quickly, and I once again forced myself back on the aircraft for what I thought was the last leg of the journey. How wrong I was!

Eight hours later, we landed in Darwin, Australia, and again I was positive I had arrived, and

Sydney was just hours away. Sitting stuck to my seat, I looked down and hour after hour, the scene below remained the same, just arid land and red-brown earth, but no houses, villages, towns or even highways. Eight long hours later, the stewardess at least announced we were approaching Sydney.

Looking down as we descended, I noticed hundreds of red tile single-storey houses, dwarfed by high-rise office buildings in the background.

The Immigration officer just took down the work address and phone number, and waved me on. I looked around expectantly for Jennie, but couldn't see her.

"Are you Julie?" someone asked.

"Yes", I replied, turning around, to see a young dark-haired girl, looking similar to Jennie, but younger.

"Well, I am Jennie's friend, and she had to leave town on business, and asked me to come and pick you up, get you settled and show you around."

She stuck out her hand in a friendly gesture.

"Hi, my name is Sandra."

She immediately took charge, hailed a taxi, and took me to a small local hotel in King's cross. Stepping out of the taxi, I stared around at the streams of people casually walking the sidewalks. The blinking bars, restaurants, night-clubs and neon lights, reminded me vividly of Soho, London.

Checking around the hotel room, peering through the curtains of my room, I watched, fascinated at the relaxed style of a very diverse and casual group of people.

Sydney, I found to be a sophisticated city, full of "old and new" Australians walking down to Arcula Quay. I took one of their innumerable ferry trips, and stared enviously at the luxurious homes, facing their private yacht moorings.

The following weekend, Sandra took me for a short drive to see the surf carnivals. I watched, fascinated, as superbly built lifesavers marched with military precision to their various life-saving techniques, with both reel and surfboat.

She showed me the many parks, and we wandered around The Botanic Gardens, rolling down supremely to the harbour. Later that evening, we strolled along the main highways, absorbing the atmosphere, and stopping in at various pubs to sample Australia's delicious home-made brews.

I loved the laid-back atmosphere of Australia - the beautiful white sandy beaches, like Manly, surrounded by picturesque Norfolk pine trees, lying in the sun with Sandra, watching the bikinied tanned girls and the muscular men. Why, oh why, did it seem to be at the end of the world? Noticing the shark safety net, it was very comforting to see the lifesavers so close by.

Fascinated by the stories and intrigue surrounding the Aboriginees, I searched the streets trying to catch a glimpse of them. Sandra told me they were kind and gentle people. She described the women as impish and pretty, and the men were broad-nosed with curly black hair.

Sandra escorted me on a tour of the new opera house overlooking the bay. She told me it was sculptured to represent the shape of sails moving in the breeze, and as it gleamed in the sunlight, I thought what a distinctive landmark for descending Sydney planes. Her eyes sparkling with pride, she went on to say it cost $100 million, but as a symbol of Australian pride and architectural achievement, it was worth every penny.

After five days, Jennie returned to Sydney. She looked drawn and tired, and I was worried.

"You look as though you have been working too hard, Jennie."

"Well, this job entails travelling from town to town selling, and it's hard. I have to manage and train the personnel, and we lose a lot of them on completion of each trip, because it isn't easy."

Obviously, this was the job she had in mind for me, and it sure didn't sound that great, but I was here now, and I would try it out.

It didn't take long to find out the men here were very different from any I had known before. They were dominant and masculine, which was marvellous, but they treated you as one of the boys, not as a woman. Watching and participating in everything from pubbing to sports, I noticed the men spent most of their time either in a pub or involved in a sporting event with their male buddies. After the courteous and gentlemanly manners of the Middle Eastern men, it was a rude awakening.

One evening, I waited for my date to appear. I had dressed up in a pink dress and high heels. In walked my date, in shorts and wearing no shoes. He walked to the car, got in and took off. If I had waited for him to open my door, I would still be standing there! At the pub, there was no question as to what I would like to drink, I was just handed a schooner of, of course, beer. This was a complete change.

The rest of the day, a crowd of us took off in Jennie's station wagon for our first sales trip. After the first day, I soon found how hard the job really was. A group of about 8 girls would be dropped off at an assigned spot, and we walked the beat until 5:30 p.m. It was exhausting, nerve-wracking, and tedious, to say the least.

I soon found out after our motel and meals were paid for, we made little or no money, it was absurd. The only people who benefitted were the managers, and Jennie was one of them, but for me, it was a complete waste of time.

Chatting over cocktails one evening back again in Sydney, I confessed to Jennie I would not be going on their next trip, as I didn't like it, and I didn't make any money. She understood, but suggested as she had some vacation time due, we try to visit the capital Canberra, and take a tour of the famous Australian outback. Looking over at her, sitting so tall, elegant and composed, it was difficult for me to visualize her comatose and near death.

"Jennie", I asked cautiously, "What eventually happened between you and Shahada?"

She looked pained by the memory.

"You know how much I loved him, but he was quite blunt in the end, and he told me he would never marry me. The last I heard, he married the girl his parents chose for him, so I hope he is happy" she said bitterly.

She ordered another drink, and I dropped the subject quickly.

She told me she could leave in a few days for our trip. She suggested we drive to Canberra first, and from there, make our way to Broken Hill and the outback country.

Taking Jennie's station wagon, laden with supplies and emergency equipment for any breakdowns, we drove off on our unchartered adventure. Driving into Canberra, I immediately noticed its quiet serene quality and architectural organization. A man-made lake centered the town, and visiting Parliament House, adjacent to the shore of Lake Burley Griffin, I saw it faced the National War Memorial, which shimmed in the distance. We stopped for a pleasant lunch at Black Mountain, and then drove west.

Endless miles of scrub continued until we approached the ancient River Darling, which flows from the Eastern Mountains and the Queensland border to the Murray River on the Victorian border. A town, Jennie told me, owing its existence to the fabled silver, lead and zinc mines, started last century. The Broken Hill area was full of wombats, goannas, kockubuna, emus, and kangaroos, and other fascinating and intriguing wildlife.

Returning East towards Sydney, Jennie decided to show me more of the Western plains of New South Wales. This was sheep country, and she wanted to give me the opportunity to also see the great red kangaroo.

We took a tour of a genuine sheep station, "The Mole", near Dubbo. We were just in time to watch the sheep shearing, and be amazed at the intelligent and uncanny ability of the sheepdogs. Gazing up into the trees, I spotted a koala bear and nearby, grazing

141

peacefully, kangaroos. Other sightseers recommended we visit the Western Plains Zoo where all the animals from all over the world roamed unrestricted, but we decided to continue our trip.

The time flew by, and driving back along the dusty roads, I got quite used to seeing the loping kangaroos casually hopping across the roads. After a long and tiring drive, we eventually re-entered Sydney and felt the brash and exhilarating upbeat atmosphere of the city.

I was sad to leave Jennie and Sydney, but this was not the long-lost country I was seeking, and it was time to return to Beirut...

CHAPTER TWENTY~SIX

I took up my life again in Beirut, as before, and was lucky to find a good job with another American firm, Armco Steel Corporation. Valerie and her husband, Ralph, moved into a new apartment, and I returned back to the old social scene.

The Grandparents calmed down a lot, and tried not to interfere, and came over every Sunday to visit Darren and Tarek. I would in turn also visit them, and leave the boys there overnight. I could now converse in Arabic which alleviated a lot of misunderstandings. There were still many obstacles and barriers to overcome, but we compromised, and made it as painless as possible.

Having Valerie in Beirut was like having a long-lost sister, and I was thankful for our chance meeting on the Tabarja Beach, when I met her and Tracey. I could talk to her about anything, and I dreaded the thought that one day, Ralph's company would send them to another country, or back to England.

We all spent great weekends and fun times in the mountains skiing in the beautiful resorts. The nearest one was only about twenty minutes driving time away by car, a scenic route of winding, hilly, green mountains. Memories of the beautiful countryside and beauty of the hills and the incredible cedar trees of Lebanon, I knew would always remain with me.

Most of our days were spent on the beach, and we all glowed with good health and tan. My office in the summer months opened at 7 a.m., and closed at 2 p.m. I would rush back to the apartment, pick up the boys, and head for the beach, and eat a leisurely lunch, with Valerie, overlooking the ocean. How long would this life continue? Of course, I hoped, forever ...

My second warning of impending trouble in fabulous Beirut happened in small incidences.

One evening in 1970, I was out on a date with a handsome Army officer, and was peacefully enjoying a very good film in one of the cinemas in Ras Beirut. The film abruptly stopped, and everyone began screaming hysterically, and started pushing and shoving to get out.

I looked at Khalil in genuine alarm.

"Is there a bomb in the cinema?" I shouted, clasping his arm for moral support.

"I don't know what it could be" he answered, looking very worried.

We were literally caught up in the rushing mass of pushers, and were carried outside by the mass of bodies. We thankfully breathed in the cool night air, and as I looked around, I saw hordes of young men with sticks and weapons of all kinds, running amok breaking anything and everything in sight. They were hitting windows, signs, doors, flower pots and cars. As we both walked cautiously to Khalil's car, I saw a scrawny young man with his arms raised, just about to strike the windshield. Just as he was about to swing, Khalil rushed up and knocked the stick out of his hand.

At the sight of his uniform and holster, he backed off immediately, babbling something in Arabic, and ran off down the street.

"What did he say, Khalil? What is wrong, why are they doing this?"

"He said Nasser is dead, I can't believe it" he replied, in a shocked tone.

"Is that a good enough reason to destroy everything in sight?" I asked, in surprise.

"This is our way of showing grief" he replied. I nodded, remembering well, and we clamoured into his car.

Driving home, tires were burning in the street, and broken glass was everywhere. Hysterical, uncontrolled people were rampaging through the streets, screaming and shouting, but Khalil – very calm and controlled- drove around all the obstacles with cool precision.

At last, safe and sound, we arrived at my apartment. He gallantly escorted me personally inside my front door to make sure I was safe, and excused himself as he needed to return to headquarters to help clear the streets, and try to stop the useless damage. I kissed him warmly, and he bolted back to his car.

It seemed from then on, things were never quite the same. A feeling of uneasiness and fear swept throughout the city. You could feel it in the atmosphere, the furtive glances, eyes quickly averted from yours, and your own responsive quickening of your footsteps.

Talking on the phone to the rest of my friends, they felt the same tension and fear, but Joanne and Valerie laughed it off.

"It will pass like all the other disturbances." Valerie said.

About a month later, I was visiting Emmina, my sister-in-law. She was a small lady, with a large heart of gold, who besides having eight children of varying ages of her own, managed to work as a dressmaker all day.

We were sitting down chatting, enjoying some strong Arabic coffee and sweet cakes, when a burst of gunfire silenced us abruptly. We looked at each other in fright. All eight of of Emmina's children ran outside screaming, followed closely by Tarek, Jr. and Darren. Cautiously straining our necks, we peered over the wall outside the house, to attempt to see where the gunfire was originating. More shells and gunfire broke out, and we scrambled quickly back in, as this time, it sounded closer. We all huddled together in the sitting room in protective closeness, and tried to maintain a normal conversation, vainly trying to blot out the increasing sound of gunfire and explosives.

This went on for a couple of hours, and then a sudden silence surrounded us. We looked at each other hopefully. I jumped up quickly.

"Well, Emmina, perhaps it's safe now to try and get home."

"Please be very careful, Julie. My parents will kill me if anything happens to you and the boys."

Privately, I knew they wouldn't have worried about me, but they would have about the boys. After another hour of relative calm and gunfire, I decided to take a chance and attempt to drive back. Scurrying with the two boys to my faithful little MG, with

Emmina's voice still ringing in my ears to be careful, I took off.

I meandered my way around the back roads, keeping away from the main boulevards, watching closely for any disturbances or gunfire. Turning into the next street, my heart lurched. Straight ahead of me, two burning tires were in the middle of the road, and a crowd of angry looking wild-eyed people were gathered around the fire.

I couldn't return, so I turned to the boys and told them quietly, we were going to have some fun, and run over those tires ahead of us in the road. Firmly, I instructed them to crouch down as far as they could in the backseat, and be quiet. I revved up the engine, put it in gear, and ran straight over the burning tires, not looking right or left.

A few days later, Valerie called.

"I'm afraid I have some bad news, Julie." My heart sank. I knew one day this would come. My fears were confirmed as she told me they were being transferred out of Beirut, and re-assigned to live in England, for at least two years. Valerie was devastated, she also adored Beirut. It was a place you either hated or loved, you either couldn't wait to leave, or you wanted to stay forever.

She became more and more despondent as the day of her departure grew closer, and once more, I made the farewell trip to the airport. I watched sadly as they all walked across the tarmac to their waiting plane. I was going to miss her, we were so close. She was a person who knew everything about my life, a special friend to confide in.

CHAPTER TWENTY~SEVEN

The years flew by, and Darren and Tarek, Jr., fluent now in both Arabic and English, were now small young men of 6 and 7 years of age.

One particularly sunny Sunday, I decided to do some shopping along Hamra Street, the fashionable European section of Beirut, where Paris-like cafes and exclusive boutiques flourished. Walking out of the beauty salon, after having the luxury of a pedicure and shampoo and set, I felt really beautiful and pampered.

Walking slowly down the street, admiring the clothes and shoes in the shop windows, a sudden explosion or noise brought me to a start. I glanced back, and could see in the distance, some sort of parade or demonstration coming towards me. As if by magic, everyone on the street disappeared. I looked around, alarmed. As it got closer and closer, I could make out all the soldiers carrying machine guns and seemed to be jumping up and down, shouting and gesturing in a very frightening manner. I couldn't understand any words, so I continued walking at my same leisurely pace.

I jumped with fright as a hand touched my shoulder. Standing behind me in the doorway, was a bespectacled, frightened old man peering anxiously at me.

"You had better get off the street" he murmured in English. "If you know what's good for you."

"No, I will not. I will continue to the end of Hamra Street", I answered.

This time, he replied in Arabic, thinking I wouldn't understand.

"Mashnoon" he said. (This means "crazy" in Arabic).

"La, Mish Mashnoon", I replied. (No, I was not). He looked surprised, and I left him crouched down in the shop entrance, behind a sturdy archway.

I continued walking, and refused to turn my head as the parade caught up with me. As it passed by, I looked up, and they looked surprised to see the lone pedestrian, and mockingly pointed their machine guns at me. I froze inside, turned away, and continued my steady pace until they were out of sight.

Things seemed to quiet down again, and soon it was Christmas. I missed Valerie so much, and received an invitation from her to visit for the holidays. As Tarek's father was co-guardian with me, I needed to obtain his permission to leave the country with the children, so I picked up a cab and went over there.

Shariffa greeted me suspiciously, and I explained to Mahmood in their language that the children and I would like to spend Christmas in England with Valerie and her family. Shariffa started her usual screaming fit, but Mahmood understood and promised he would obtain the required paper the following day.

My close boyfriend for some time now, was an attractive Armenian, Hagop Rachanian, whose family left Turkey some time ago, and in Lebanon, they proved to be valuable and hard workers. From these humble beginnings, he now managed three fashionable shoe stores in the Hamra area, and would take many trips to Paris and Rome, to buy the latest designs and fashions.

I was very fond of Hagop, but remembering Jennie's tragic experience, kept it well hidden. His family, I knew, were arranging for him to meet suitable Armenian girls, unmarried and unencumbered, and I realized the situation from both sides was hopeless.

Our trips out together, Darren and Tarek, Jr. in tow, were vivid reminders of past outings with Tarek, and Hagop's caring and devotion to children was heart-rendering.

A few days before Christmas, Hagop took us to the airport for our trip to London. After the usual long and tiresome ride with two active and excited boys, I looked anxiously around for my long-lost sister. I suddenly saw her walking towards me, and we rushed to embrace, walking and talking non-stop as we left the airport.

Along with high unemployment, the buses were also on strike, so it took us about three hours to even arrive at the railway station. Another two hours of travelling until we got to her house, and it seemed longer and more troublesome to get there, than it had from Beirut to London.

In spite of the snow and ice-bound roads, the time spent together was worth it, reminiscing and giggling about the good times we spent together, the many shared memories recaptured again.

Darren, Tarek Jr., and Tracey spent the afternoon playing with snowballs, and building a snowman, and the boys were thrilled at their first glimpse of snow, thank goodness, not remembering their last miserable trip to England.

Time ran out too quickly and now it became Valerie's turn to say goodbye at the airport. Running late, we dashed along the endless corridors, Tarek clutching fast onto his new Christmas present, bought on Oxford Street – a large cuddly teddy bear, by far his favourite present.

Back to work again, and more signs of conflict and turmoil...

Working peacefully in the office one afternoon, a sudden roaring sound filled the air. Everyone rushed to the windows, and glimpsed with astonishment, two tanks slowing coming up the street. We quickly turned on the local radio, and found out fresh fighting had broken out in the area, and they advised everyone to stay off the street. We looked at each other in fright, but I was determined I would try to get home one way or another. More explosions could be heard in the area, and many of the office staff started shaking and crying, as they seemed even closer this time.

Closing the office door quickly, I ran out into the parking lot and jumped into my car. Slowly driving down the street, I was startled to see two tanks positioned on either side of the main thoroughfare. I screeched to a sudden stop, and then with stunned amazement watched wide-eyed as a very drunken European man proceeded to try to cross the street.

If it hadn't been so dangerous, it would have been hilarious. He must have got caught in a local bar, and somehow had no idea what was going on. Somebody was watching over him, because I observed him stagger drunkenly across the road, more gunfire took place, but miraculously, missed him completely.

Shaking my head in astonishment, I turned sharply onto a side street, which I hoped would take me home. As I drove on, I suddenly saw in front of me what appeared to be two dead bodies in the road. I weaved around them, and hoped and prayed that whoever had shot them had stopped firing. By now, shaking and driving like a maniac, I drove headlong down the street, keeping my eyes open for any gun snipers or tanks.

Not a soul could be seen, and eyes wide with fear, I eventually arrived at my apartment, and rushed into the waiting arms of my children.

This was it! I had to get out before the whole country blew up. The next day, everything went back to normal, but I knew this was only the beginning of worse things to come.

Many times I thought about America, and dreamed one day there might be a chance for us all to live there. I had relatives from my Step-Grandmother's side living in Northport, a suburb of New York, and the following year, they invited me to visit. My two weeks' vacation time was due, so I left the boys in the area of Shariffa and Mahmood, who were thrilled, and took off. Stopping off in London, I was able to obtain a visa for six months. Arriving in New York, I walked into the terminal. As I looked around at the millions of rushing people, noise and hubbub, I became terrified....

What was a dime? What was a nickel?

I looked around in complete panic, trying to make a simple phone call.

"Was this the world traveller???"

I was nearly in tears by the time Pam and Roy, my relatives arrived, and we clambered into their car. I watched wide-eyed at the massive freeways and the fast-paced traffic, doubting I would ever find the courage to drive on them. It looked death-defying.

Their home was magnificent in a well maintained area. Turning on the TV, I became mesmerized by the 24-hour TV programs with about 40 channels. Used to only one French and two Arabic channels, I became addicted, and sat for days, eyes glued to the screen transfixed. Pam and Roy finally dragged me away, and took me on a few journeys into New York – once to see a Broadway play, and another for shopping and browsing.

Pam and Roy realized full well Beirut was a "hot spot", but knew if I wanted to live in the U.S.A., I would have to manage it myself. My two weeks came to a close, and Pam drove me to the airport.

Flying back over the ocean, my mind was made up. We would move to the U.S.A. one way or another. Not New York City, that place scared the hell out of me. Perhaps somewhere in California.

Relaxing and dreaming a little on the plane, listening to some wonderful ballads through my earphones, Tony Bennett began singing "I left my heart in San Francisco."

That was it ... San Francisco here I come...

CHAPTER TWENTY~EIGHT

It was a cool March day in Beirut in 1971 when I left for San Francisco. I was used to not knowing anyone, so this did not matter. It was now or never – the tension in Beirut was mounting, I could feel instinctively everything could just blow up at any minute.

I told the Grandparents I was going for a holiday and left the boys with them, and they were thrilled, I am sure hoping I would not come back. Again getting the practically free tickets from TMA, via PAN AM made it possible.

The flight over in a new Jumbo Jet was exciting, and the service, meals and comfort was nothing less than superb. I had given myself three months to get settled, find a job, an apartment and return. Although I had a six month visitor's visa, I needed this time to return to Beirut to pick up the children, before the visa expired. We stopped off in Los Angeles for our baggage inspection, visa, and passport formalities, and at last, we were back on our original plane, bound for San Francisco.

Looking down from the window seat, it certainly looked a fantastic city from the air, and I felt my stomach churning as we circled over the airport. At last, we landed, and I walked out in a daze, not knowing in which direction to go. Jumping into a cab, I asked the driver to take me to a reasonable hotel, centrally located.

San Francisco – with its hills, cable cars and cosmopolitan atmosphere was a beautiful sight. The hotel, in comparison, was dull and uninteresting, and not the place to get acquainted with anyone, or begin my strategic campaign.

Glancing at the paper the following day, I noticed an advertisement for a Residence Club, I presumed, a communal-type living arrangement. For a very reasonable sum, you were given three meals a day, a comfortable room, and recreation rooms for billiards and table-tennis. Finding a telephone, I called up, and was pleased to find out they still had vacancies.

Jumping onto the first available cable car, I found it easily and walked in. I looked around with interest. A large TV room and lounge to the right, and downstairs led down to the cafeteria. A young man at the reception desk escorted me around briefly, and showed me the comfortable room and shared bathroom. The ample furnishings and pleasant surroundings pleased me, and I could see they catered to a young and obviously friendly crowd.

This was what I was looking for.

Making friends and valuable contacts was the most important thing for my survival. I soon found out I needed to obtain a Social Security Number. Talking to the other residents, I was informed after filling out the required form, this usually took around six weeks. I sure hoped my money would last that long, as I was on a tight budget. I filled out the application truthfully, and sent it off. Five or six weeks later, there it was, waiting for me in my numbered mail slot!

I began meeting many interesting people from all over, and got friendly with a very nice Canadian, Frank, who proved extremely helpful on hints of getting around and inexpensive places to eat and free things to do in the city.

The following day, eager, but nervous, I entered one of the employment offices. As was normal, I filled out the application form, and was then called in for a personal interview, to discuss my background and qualifications. She looked up quickly from her revolving files.

"I presume you have all the documents and green card necessary so you can work?"

"Of course, I have." I replied.

I waited anxiously for her to ask me to produce it, but with a quick glance at my worksheet, she hurriedly flipped through her available job list. I went through interview after interview, and then I was lucky and landed a job in a Public Relations firm, very near to the Residence Club.

The job, freedom from any ties, and San Francisco, I was enjoying, but I still felt a constant ache in my heart for my children, which could not be denied. Three months went by, and in the PR business, it was very normal to be burning the midnight oil at all hours, on special projects.

The required time elapsed, and it was now time for me to go back and get my boys out of Beirut...

The next day, I nervously entered the Manager's office. Working there only a short time, I was worried he would not give me the time off to go back to Beirut. Out of necessity, at the original interview, I made no mention of having any children, as I knew the position would not be offered to me if they knew the truth.

Mr. Luthenthal was an older grey-haired Jewish gentleman, stern but humourous, and he smiled warmly as I entered. I sat down, and began to tell him my story

"Why didn't you tell me this before, Julie?" he asked.

"Well, I knew I wouldn't have been offered the job if I had told you this, isn't that right?" He nodded slowly.

"Well, as you know, Julie, there are a lot of long hours and overtime with this job, and very difficult for someone with young children."

I went on to them him I really needed two weeks' vacation to give me time to go back to Lebanon, sell my furniture and leave again. He reluctantly agreed to my two weeks' vacation without pay, and just as I was closing the door, I remembered one very important question I forgot to mention.

"One more thing, Mr. Luthenthal. Will you promise to keep my job open until I return, so at least I have this to rely on when I return, as I have nothing else as a back-up."

"Alright, that's the least I can do for you" he replied.

He advised me to make sure accommodation was ready and waiting for my children when I returned, and I assured him I was already looking for an apartment. He wished me luck and the following day, I was winging my way once more back to Lebanon. Going back and forth was becoming a habit. It seemed perfectly natural and normal to me now.

Thankful to see Darren and Tarek again, I held them close, vowing never to leave them ever again, and so happy I found a country where we could live.

The following morning after my arrival in Beirut, I called Joanne on the phone. She told me things were getting worse, as more and more demonstration and uprisings were occurring on a regular basis.

I met her later in the evening at her apartment, and sat down again on the familiar balcony, and sipped our usual white Chablis.

Now the children could speak Arabic fluently, I didn't dare tell them we were leaving for America. Being so young, they would have been so excited, and as soon as they saw Shariffa and Mahmoud, would have blurted it out in childish innocence.

Visiting Emmina and the children for the last time was heartbreaking, but there was no choice but to remain silent. I would have liked to have told her, but knew I could not, and looking back one last time as we left, I felt sure I would never ever see her or her children again.

The last night before my departure, Joanne and I made arrangements to spend it together at our favourite nightclub, "Caves Du Roy".

She looked fantastic in a strapless red dress, and I poured myself into an off-the-shoulder black outfit. We both sat on our well-worn bar stools, and ordered champagne.

"I never believed you could do it, Julie, but you did, and not a moment too soon. So many people have left, and more are leaving."

Even the bartender, a handsome Italian whose reputation of remembering everyone's particular brew years and years later, was gone, and many old friends seemed to have disappeared. Many champagnes and hours later, we sat and cried in our drinks, and staggered out of the club at 4 a.m. as the door slammed shut. This would be the last time I would ever be there again! It was a sad and final night.

The next day dawned, and bright and early, I was able at last to tell Darren and Tarek the good news. They were as excited as I knew they would be. Hagop showed up at the hotel, and as previously arranged, they were dropped off at a nearby open-air restaurant for safety. Hagop and I drove to the airport to present our tickets, and take care of the airport tax.

From habit, I looked suspiciously around for any sign of the many relatives or friends of Tarek's family, and then Hagop went off to pick up the boys from the restaurant, just before the final call for the plane would be announced. He ran out of the airport, and reappeared with two struggling, hyper-active, wildly excited children.

We looked at each other fondly and embraced. The Grandparents would be after his scalp when they found out he helped us, and I doubted I would ever see him again either. Inwardly feeling nervous, I approached the desk with my passport. The official barely looked up, stamped it, and I walked through, waving frantically to Hagop until he was out of sight.

As the plane took off, glancing down this time for the last time on Beirut, I saw billowing smoke and mortar shells exploding somewhere in the mountains. My God, it had already started; I left not a moment too soon. I prayed this was my last trip in search for a country to call home.

The long, tiresome, but exciting plane journey was over, and we arrived in San Francisco. A long line of other passengers walked quickly by without being stopped, but when he examined my passport, he asked me kindly to wait at the back.

This was it, I was going to be sent back to Beirut, and I knew it. My stomach was doing leap frogs and my legs were feeling so shaky, I sat down quickly, before I thought I might fall. In what seemed like an eternity, he slowly walked over to me and looked us over.

"Why have you come back to America? I see you were here three months ago on a visit."

"Yes, that's right, but in that time, I was lucky to meet my future husband, so I went back to pick up my two sons."

He looked very suspiciously at all of us.

"Is he here, the man you say you're going to marry?"

"Yes, I replied, he is here I am sure. I could have him paged if you like".

He looked again at the excited, expectant faces of Darren and Tarek, shrugged his shoulders, and a smile creased his face.

"No, that's okay, that won't be necessary. Good luck."

I could not believe it. As I walked away, holding onto the boys tightly, I expected any second for him to call me back, so I practically ran to the baggage area. I wanted to whoop and jump up and down, but calmly kept walking. We had made it, so far.

Frank, from the Residence Club, true to his word, was waiting in the lounge as we walked in. His promise to assist me in case the Official had asked to see him, was not necessary now, and I was glad. I warmly embraced him, and he shyly hugged the kids.

He drove us to my pre-rented apartment, and we just sat quietly celebrating my last escape and my happy arrival.

The apartment I rented was small, and from the windows of the sitting room, I could see the cable cars running up and down the street. In a few weeks, I went to register the children for school, and answered truthfully the questionnaire.

Arriving home the next evening, exhausted after a hectic day at work, Darren and Tarek handed me a note from school. Opening it up, I read the school needed a copy of my green card, or I could come by with the original. What was I going to do now?

I began to think frantically of anybody who might help, and then I remembered Rita. I met Rita at the Residence Club. She was also English, older, hardened, many times divorced and bitter, but she might be able to come up with a solution.

Talking to her on the phone that evening, she was pleased to hear from me, and asked about my recent trip. I then went on to tell her about the note from the school and the mess I was in.

"Let me see what I can do. They did say you could send a copy, right?"

"Yes, Rita, they did." She laughed.

"I have a wacky idea which might work. Call me tomorrow."

Temporarily reprieved, I put the phone down with relief, hoping she really could do something.

The following day, another note came from the school. Immediately panicking, I called the school and told them I was working a lot of overtime, but would be sending a copy as soon as possible.

Sitting in the apartment that evening, after putting two jumping jacks to bed, my doorbell rang. Opening it up, there stood a grinning Rita.

"Well, here it is, for what it's worth. I hope it works." And she presented me with a photostat of a green card with my name on it.

I invited her in, and we spent the rest of the evening gossiping and exchanging travel tips.

The next day, apprehensively, I folded it up, and handled it to the boys.

CHAPTER TWENTY~NINE

That evening, and for many to come, I jumped at the sound of the doorbell and phone, and expected any second for someone from the school to call to say they knew it was a fake.

Time and work continued, and the job in the PR firm, increased tenfold, and I realized I could not keep the hours required, and take care of the children. I needed to find another job with normal hours, so I could arrive home in reasonable time to make them supper, and put them to bed.

San Francisco's windy days and cool nights reminded me a lot of England, and visiting China Town, plus all the intriguing and fascinating areas, made it a fun city to live in.

I again started job hunting, and made an application to a shipping company working for the President, and out of 50 applicants, was lucky to be chosen. In the interview, the question of the green card was again brought up, but I smiled and said:

"Oh, yes of course."

I had been working for about six months and loved my job and loved my Boss, he was wonderful to me and I could get home by at least 5:30 each day for the boys. After school they would play pool at a nearby boys club and wait for my return.

A few days later, I received a letter from Valerie. They were now living in Dallas, Texas and Tracey and her would be coming to San Francisco to visit me, and would be arriving next weekend. To see my closest friend again was the tonic I needed. I couldn't wait to show her around San Francisco, and take her to my office on the 11th floor. I was astonished to find in my particular building, there really wasn't any 13th floor, due to superstitions connected with the number 13, and San Francisco's history of earthquakes.

The boys jumped up and down excitedly when I told them Valerie and Tracey would be coming, as growing up together for so many years, there were very close.

The cable car stopped right outside the apartment building, so it only took me about 15 minutes in the morning to get to work. A few days later, smiling broadly at the thought of my visitor, I was called into the manager's office.

His expression looked grim, and as soon as he asked me to sit down, I knew something was wrong. He looked directly into my eyes and said:

"Do you have a green card, Julie?"

"Well, Dave, it's not with me now, I leave it at home for safe keeping, but I can get it for you", just biding time, not even thinking straight.

"Well, why don't you get it then", Dave said.

Slowly walking back to my desk, I knew there was no way I was going to explain this away. Somebody must have told him, or the Immigration Department had caught up with me. It was just better to tell the truth. I walked back into his office and shut the door.

"I'm sorry Dave, it's no good to lie anymore. I don't have a green card."

He looked at me blankly.

"Why didn't you tell us this before?"

"Well, let's face it, you would not have been able to hire me, if I had told you. How did you find out?"

Dave looked puzzled.

"It was very strange. A lady with an accent called up and said she was from the Immigration Department, and informed us we had a lady named Julie working here without proper identification. She left her name and number. When I returned the call, the Immigration Department told me they did not have anyone of that name working there."

I shook my head in bewilderment.

"This looks more like a personal vendetta, somebody who knows me personally, and knows also I don't have a green card, wouldn't you agree?"

Dave nodded his head.

"It sure does, but the problem is Julie, as the President is away right now, I will have to let you go until I have talked this over with him, and see what we are going to do about it. I'm sorry."

Nodding numbly, tears streaming down my face, I packed up my personal belongings, and rushed out of the office.

Walking despondently into the apartment, I stopped dead. There stood Valerie, very surprised to see me. We ran into each other's arms.

"How did you get in? It's wonderful to see you!"

"The landlady let me in. Luckily, you told her you were expecting me. How is it you are back so early, I wasn't expecting you until after 5 p.m."

I sat down slowly into the old overstuffed armchair and sighed.

"Well, Val, it's like this ..."

After relating the whole story to her detail by detail, neither of us were any closer to an answer.

In a few hours, the boys burst through the doors like tornadoes, nearly running down Valerie and Tracey in their excitement, and we sat down to dinner together, just like so many old times in Beirut.

Later in the evening, talking it over and going through the few people whom I knew were aware of my circumstances, one thing Dave told me suddenly resurfaced. I remembered distinctly he told me the woman on the phone had an accent. The only person I knew was Rita, and actually the more I thought about it, she was the only who knew all this information. That was it, but would she turn me in? I felt I knew the reason. She was jealous of my friendship with another girlfriend of hers, and as we were closer in age and got on better together, and being older, she felt the odd one out, and did this to try to get rid of me.

The next day was cool and windy, so we decided to go out together, and I would show her the sights and sounds of good old San Francisco. Taking the cable car, we walked down to the Wharf, and breathed in the scintillating smells of live lobsters and crabs, and watched the strolling musicians. We happily paid our fare, and stepped onto the ferry for our short trip around the Bay, revelling in the scenery.

Tracey dragged us into the local fair, and I watched them, faces as white as sheets, and hair streaming around their faces, zooming around on the Figure 8. After a wonderful fun-ridden exhausting day, we all arrived back at the apartment, and both throwing our shoes off, sank down on my lumpy old sofa.

I made the most of her stay, and tried not to worry or think about my plight. Nothing was going to spoil her visit.

Leaving Val and Tracey at the airport was upsetting, and as I returned to the apartment, I knew some new decisions would have to be made... I telephoned a German boyfriend of mine, Elmar, who owned a home of his own, and who had extra accommodation, and told him about my desperate situation, and he kindly invited us to stay. It was possible for me to get temporary secretarial work, but the hourly wage would not cover the rent and food. I found a summer camp for the boys for a few weeks, as school was already over, which would give me more time to get myself and my finances together.

A couple of months passed, and one day, I received a phone call from Dave, the manager of the Shipping Company.

"What are you doing tomorrow, Julie?"

"Well, Dave, luckily, I have a temporary job to go to tomorrow. Why?"

"No, you don't. You are coming back here tomorrow. Mr. Handy and I talked it over, and we will fix something up for you."

With a singing heart, I put down the telephone, and hoped everything would be straightened out.

CHAPTER THIRTY

Going back was a joy to me, and everyone was happy and delighted I was back. The President and Manager called me into their office, and began discussing various possibilities available for me. They suggested first of all for me to go to the Immigration Department and renew my visitor's visa.

Walking slowing along Sansome Street the following day, I soon found the right department. I presented my passport, and enquired about extending my visa.

He shook his head slowly.

"I'm sorry, we cannot renew it."

"What are the possibilities of getting a work permit?" I enquired.

"I'm sorry, unless there is something you can do that no other American can, it's impossible."

It looked pretty hopeless, but I kept on trying.

"What about if someone sponsors me into the country?" I asked desperately.

"That is difficult, and perhaps it takes a year, and of course, in the meantime, you cannot work."

I smiled and nodded.

He got up and walked around the desk and quietly said:

"Do you have a boyfriend?" I thought, what a nerve, and what business is it of his?

"Well, if he is an American get married. That is the only safe way of being able to stay here." He winked at me secretly, and went back to his work.

I left the department despondently, realizing this was not possible for me, as all my boyfriends were foreigners. Back at the office, I told the boss the news. He smiled mischievously.

"Well, if that is that they told you to do. Let's get on with it."

I looked at him in astonishment.

"That's not going to be easy, with two children."

"You know nothing is impossible, Julie, we'll get something arranged for you."

A few days later, the dreaded official letter arrived from Immigration, telling me I had to leave the country in ten days; otherwise, they would come and pick me up. Ten days – this was too much. What would I do now? Rushing into the boss's office as soon as I got in the next morning, I told him the bad news.

"We will all help as much as we can to stop you having to leave" he assured me. He looked so positive, as though it was a very easy and simple task.

The days crept by one by one, and I spent sleepless nights, awakening from frightening nightmares, where I was being handcuffed and escorted out of the country, with two desolate crying children walking beside me .Then being flown back to Beirut, and being handed over to the grinning Grandparents, Ali, the eldest brother, standing behind them with his gun.

I would visible jump when the doorbell or telephone rang, and was a nervous wreck.

The following week, the President called me in, and said it was possible a friend of his had found a man who would cooperate and help me. I looked at him, shocked.

"When can I meet this good Samaritan?" I asked eagerly.

"He will meet you tomorrow at 8 p.m. at "Chez Pauls".

"Didn't he want anything in return?" I asked enquiringly.

"No, nothing. He is just a nice guy who wants to help someone out."

I waited nervously for our meeting and sat tensely looking around, until I saw a young, long-haired, jean-clad man approach me. At least ten years younger than I??? Oh my God.

"Are you Julie?" he enquired.

"Yes, I said. Are you the man Dave sent me to meet?"

"Yes, that's me." I am Kenneth"

He sat down and leaning confidently towards me, said:

"I heard about you and the hard life and knocks you have gone through, and was told you are a good person, who only wants the best opportunities for yourself and the boys, so if I can help in any way, I will."

We chatted on, and found out a little more about each other, and I explained we only had about three days left to get married.

"Well, let's get on with it" he said, "I'm ready."

"Let's do it tomorrow. We can drive up to Reno in my car and get the license and get married." I could not believe my ears – this was actually going to happen.

Sleeping a little better that night, I was positive he would have a change of heart and not show up, and I was mentally prepared for it. But, as promised, exactly on time, he drove up in his old beat up Volkswagen, smiling bravely.

Even though it wasn't the "Wedding of the Year", and I was no Princess, and he was certainly no Prince, I put on a long dress and attractive top, but he on the other hand, looked as though he was going on a hike. Who cares, he was here. We must have made an unusual pair.

It seemed I was fated to have unusual marriages, either weird, unbelievable or not understandable...

Arriving in Reno after the short drive, we walked into the first marriage chapel on the route. Kenneth walked briskly to the desk and told the Clerk we wanted to get married. Hardly glancing up from his paperwork, he told us to take a seat and someone would be with us in a few minutes.

Looking around the commercialized wedding chapel, I was thankful to see we did not look as unusual as I thought. Many odd looking couples, some with screaming dirty kids running amok, and many women in advanced stages of pregnancy. Ken was told where to obtain the licence, and we took off. It only took a few minutes, and sitting down again, she told us we were right after a little old couple, who were gazing into each other's eyes with obvious adoration, what a trip this was, was I dreaming again...

Walking into the chapel, we were greeted by the first Black Priest I have ever seen. The words of the ceremony began, and then he came to the crucial question.

Turning to Kenneth, he asked him:

"Do you take this woman to be your lawfully wedded wife?"

Kenneth answered very casually.

"Sure", he answered. I wondered if that was even legal, but the Priest continued without a pause....

"I will" I answered in a low voice. Was this really happening?

Ken kissed me lightly on the lips, and hand-in-hand, we left. We stopped for a light dinner in Reno before heading back to San Francisco, and later he dropped me at Elmar's house.

The weeks and months passed by, and the big day arrived, or I hoped it was. Another official letter arrived from the Immigration Department, informing me to report to the office. Really fearing the worst, I stepped into the office.

Smiling broadly, they presented me with three green cards – one for Darren, one for Tarek, and one for myself.

I stared at him in shock ... and ran from the office on a cloud of heaven.

CHAPTER THIRTY~ONE

I knew we had to leave San Francisco as it was just too expensive, and I had heard that Texas was the place to be for single mothers with children, as it was cheaper to live, and also some people were even able to buy homes for themselves.

I packed up a few things that I had and hired a U-haul and made arrangements to leave San Francisco. It was with a lot of sadness that we left.

We drove first of all to San Antonio, the boys changing the gears on the truck, and poor Tarek hiding outside until we had registered, and then we would get him up to the room quietly, when I did not have enough money for two kids. It was a nightmare, but through unbelievable lightning and thunderstorms, we eventually came to San Antonio. I did not know anybody of course, what is new? But somehow, found a place to live, and by sheer luck, employment in a local radio station as the Secretary to the President ... sounded familiar to me.

The job was not very exciting, but I had to keep working. I had a small car and was still paying payments on it, missed one, so one morning waking up, went out to no car ...they had picked it up. I was not in town and no buses, so could not even get to my job. More problems, what else?

I went to the auto place where they had stored the car and paid some of the back money, and eventually, thank God, I got my car back. What a relief, at least I could get to the grocery store again.

Two years of hell ensued in San Antonio, with lots of cockroaches, no fridges, bad neighbours and scary incidents onc particular one driving on the highway, and a man trying to cut me off, really frightened me, and I speeded up to the nearest base I could see and drove up to the gates, and told the guards my problem. I thought that was enough of San Antonio, and decided that that my last hurrah would be Dallas, Texas. It would be my last chance for the family, and I knew I could not move anymore.

Again, the U-Haul, plus I had flown over to Dallas to find an apartment in Irving, and was looking forward to being able to work again and send the boys to school.

Another nightmare trip, U-Haul with a car hanging on the back of it. The boys again changing the gears, and unfortunately we got on to LBJ at the rush hour and the car started to fall off the hook. Shouting obscenities and horns blazing from the drivers stuck in the traffic jam, Darren and Tarek tried to get the car back on to the U-Haul. By some kind of miracle, the boys managed to rehook the car...

As we arrived at the apartment, actual snow was on the ground. I had never imagined snow in Dallas. We parked in front of the apartment, went in, and decided that we would move in tomorrow, as we were exhausted, and all slept peacefully on at least, a carpeted floor. It was too much to move in that night.

The next morning, I went to many secretarial office placements, and started to do temporary secretarial work, so I could get to know the city. I enrolled the boys in the local high school. They had to walk as they lived too close to the school, but that was fine, at least they were legal...

The years passed by, the boys worked as newspaper carriers, door-to-door sales, etc., and had already earned an award for selling more papers in San Antonio – an award that gave them a trip to Disneyland.

Many times, Darren had played poker in Dallas and had helped pay the rent. They are incredible boys. They both worked hard, and have been helping me since age 10. Lots of shitty jobs, time clocks, car breakdowns, daily life existence, moving again, more love life fiascos, and just day to day survival.

And life goes on ... sometimes more shitty.

I married a guy from Texas and we moved into a house in Carollton, Texas, with help from my son, as both of them were now in business for themselves in the home improvement business. It all seemed dreamlike and wonderful, of course, at the beginning. In fact, we had a beach wedding in Galveston, Texas. On our wedding day, he insisted on going on a fishing trip, and I was sick the whole time...great honeymoon, he was a hoot???

On one of my trips with my husband, I had made a ferry trip to Playa del Carmen, Mexico, and as I looked at the aquamarine water and the white sand, I said:

"One day, I will retire here."

I had fallen in love with the place on sight.

My marriage to Andrew was going down the tube after ten years, and I felt I needed to get out of Dallas, and move to my dream location. We agreed on that, and I rented out the house in Texas and took my chances in Playa del Carmen, Mexico. I went with my small little half Chihuahua doggie, Zoe, and set out on another journey to another foreign country. Another new adventure!!!

I had a lot of problems finding a place for a dog, but after many searches, I eventually found a place to stay. It was a little sparse, but I did have TV and was close to the beach.

At 62, would I be able to adapt to Mexican culture, as I had to the Lebanese, or would it be too hard.

After a couple of years, I realized I loved the place and was very happy here and made many friends. It was a difficult place to live. Plenty of people came with stars in their eyes and money in their pockets, some made it big, others left with their tails between their legs, not being able to handle the culture and the laws.

It is a very transient place, and I have seen many hundreds of people come and go in my nine years here. My sons come down quite a lot, and fell in love with the place too.

We decided to invest here, and take another big risk in our lives, so I sold my house to my son, and we brought the house together. We found a lovely place and I have been living in the villa for the last 7 years with visits from both my sons and grandchildren – all five of them.

I had a trip to Dallas in 2009 for the Christmas holidays and it had become really cold. I only had swimsuits and shorts in Playa, so had to buy a couple of things for the cold weather.

We were all sitting around in Darren's house, and I did not have a robe to wear. Suddenly, he came out with a red silk robe. I looked at it in horror.

"What is that? Where did you get it Darren?"

I was in shock, and could not understand who had given it to him and why not me, then I understood, the eldest son!

I brought it close to me, and could still smell my lost love's scent, even after 45 years, even with the old hole in the sleeve I never sewed up ... and a similar shiver went through my whole body ...

It was Kismet again...

THE END

EPILOGUE

It's now June, 2011, and in the humidity and heat of Playa Del Carmen, Mexico, I look at the beautiful aquamarine water and white sands, and I feel at home and reminisce about Beirut, Lebanon.

I dance twice a week at the best place in town "Captain Dave's" on 5th and 4th where you can inhale the sea aroma around you and have a clear view of Cozumel from your favourite bar stool in the large palapa, and listen to JJ and his great band, "BAD BOYS"!!!

Looking fondly around at the Mexican people, so warm and family oriented, so like the Lebanese people, I wonder, it seems my life is obviously destined to be in places that have intrigue and problems but I feel as safe here now, as I once did in Beirut, or Dallas, Texas.

I hope I do not have to do any more moving, that is already old, I want to die here and be buried near the sea...

I still miss my Arab love daily; I look at his pictures in my sitting room and the one taken on Hamra Street, Beirut when I was pregnant with Darren

I think about that fateful day on the beach in Beirut in 1961, and my answer that day...

…If I had known the future, the heartache, survival as a single parent in a foreign world, the wild emotional rollercoaster, would I have married that beautiful man from Beirut?

Love is international, interracial, and non-religious. It crosses all boundaries, all hearts and all colours.

I would have said "Yes"

I am proud to say I have been an American citizen for the last 30 years, and do not regret bringing my small sons to America in 1972 from Beirut. Illegal, but still, so far, the best country in the world...

I sometimes wonder if it was a dream. I look at his pictures in my wonderful home in Playa del Carmen, and then look at my two sons, and grandchildren and realize, it was not a dream, it was, MY LIFE which I lived to the full.

NO REGRETS

NOTES FROM THE AUTHOR AS TO THE AUTHENTICITY OF 'THE RED SILK ROBE"

- ❖ Documents can be obtained from Trans Mediterrenean Airways, Beirut and the UK as to the actual date of my late husband's death to be December 12th, 1963.
- ❖ Daily Express, London ''2,000 mile flight from luxury by ex showgirl Julie" 1964
- ❖ Daily Mail "Wife of vanished Pilot begs for new Search" 1963
- ❖ Dallas Morning News by Bob St John "A long search for a home leads to Dallas" 1982
- ❖ Bristol Evening Post "Julie's Story" 1980.
- ❖ Married in July 61 by Sheikh in Beirut (I am sure no records of that as destroyed through numerous civil wars)
- ❖ Marriage certificate in the Registrar's office, Bristol UK April 1962.
- ❖ Birth certificate of Darren in Bristol UK Maternity Hospital July 6th, 1962.
- ❖ Birth certificate in the French Hospital Beirut for Tarek, Jr. September 15th, 1963.

Twenty years ago, I contacted Oprah Winfrey, and she did get back to me, but wanted, of course, authenticity of my life, then it was not possible, now with the new technology it is available...

To contact me directly please feel free to write me at redsilkrobe@hotmail.com   *Thank you, Julia*

Picture of Julia Kent with her dog Zoe in 2011